Death Rider

When mountain man Rufas Kane stumbles across the body of a harmless cowboy on a hillside overlooking the spirited town of Death, the question everybody is asking themselves is: why would anyone want to kill Dan Cooper?

When one of Gene Adams's cowboys is killed in a gunfight with the ruthless Trey Skinner, it becomes apparent that Skinner is the man responsible for Cooper's untimely death. But all is not as it seems.

As the night goes on, an alarming spate of killings shakes the town to its foundations, but Gene Adams vows to find the answer and the killer before dawn or die in the attempt.

Death Rider

Boyd Cassidy

A Black Horse Western

ROBERT HALE · LONDON

© Boyd Cassidy 2010
First published in Great Britain 2010

ISBN 978-0-7090-8962-9

Robert Hale Limited
Clerkenwell House
Clerkenwell Green
London EC1R 0HT

www.halebooks.com

Typeset by
Derek Doyle & Associates, Shaw Heath
Printed and bound in Great Britain by
CPI Antony Rowe, Chippenham and Eastbourne

*Dedicated to my daughter Suzi Maria with love
and a million heartfelt blessings*

PROLOGUE

The man had thought he was alone on the side of the mountain when he piled kindling on top of his small campfire. He had seen the sun set without any fear that there was anyone else up on the side of the mountain close to the tree line. As the fire grew more intense he watched the sizzling pound of bacon in his blackened skillet start to look like the feast he knew it would be. Wearily he inhaled its aroma and swallowed the saliva which filled his mouth. Dan Cooper was a cowboy who had spent the previous three days rounding up stray steers from the woodland before sending them back down to the fertile range beyond the sprawling town.

From his high vantage point he could see the lights of the town below him. They glowed like a million fireflies and brightened the otherwise dark valley.

Cooper had already spread out his bedroll next to his saddle, close to the warmth of the fire. With his saddle as a pillow he knew that there would be few of his fellow cowboys who would have a more peaceful night's sleep than he. Riding the mountainside and finding stray steers was a lonely job, but better than most of the alternatives. Cooper liked being his own boss, doing what he had always done.

An hour earlier he had tethered his quarter horse to the trunk of a tree and watered the sturdy animal. The day had been long and hard and he looked forward to resting his bones and sleeping until sunup. As the cowboy flipped the bacon he thought that this was going to be just another night like so many others he had enjoyed over the years.

He stared down into the darkness at the lights and licked his lips. Cooper could almost taste the whiskey he knew was already flowing down there. His gloved left hand manoeuvred the coffee pot in the red-hot ashes beside the skillet. He sighed. No hard liquor for him until pay day, he silently thought. Cooper drew his penknife from his coat pocket and unfolded its keen blade. He began to cut the bacon up in the spitting fat and raised a chunk to his mouth. It was hot but tasted good. Damn good.

As Cooper chewed his horse snorted behind him. The cowboy stood and looked at his mount. There were cougars in these mountains. Although he had not seen one for five or more years it was always wise to err on the side of caution.

Cooper moved to the horse. The animal had heard something and was nervous. The cowboy drew his old .44 from its holster and cocked its hammer.

He walked to the neck of the horse and stared out into the trees. Blackness could create monsters in the minds of those with imagination but Cooper was short in that area. His kind lacked the ability to see anything which was not there. He placed one hand on the nose of the horse and tried to calm the animal as his wrinkled eyes screwed up and vainly tried to see what was cloaked in shadow. For a while he neither saw nor heard anything, but then the sound of a dried twig snapping under a horse's hoof told Cooper exactly where to aim his hogleg.

'I hear you and I got my gun cocked, *amigo!*' Cooper drawled loudly. 'Who are you and what do you want? Speak up or I'll start fanning my hammer!'

'Don't shoot! I'm just a drifter.' The voice came back through the shadows. 'I seen the fire and smelled the grub. I just thought you'd have some spare vittles to share with a man down on his luck.'

Cooper was no gunman. The gun in his hand shook as he swallowed the bacon he had been chewing. He did not know the voice and had never heard an accent like it before. Although the cowboy did not know it, it was the accent of a man raised far to the east.

'You sure are lucky!' Cooper piped up. 'I could have gunned you down thinking you was a mountain lion!'

'Can I come into your camp?' the voice requested.

'Head on in,' Cooper said.

The horseman did as instructed and steered his mount out of the trees until the light of the flickering fire illuminated him and his charge. A wiser man might have realized that this rider was not dressed in trail gear. Every inch of his body was covered in black leather. From hat down to boots. But Dan Cooper was just a simple cowhand and did not suspect that this man was anything but down on his luck.

The rider eased back on his reins.

'That coffee smells real good! The bacon does too!'

'You want a cup?' Cooper asked as he kept the gun trained on the unexpected guest.

'That would be real fine!' The horseman dismounted and tied his reins to the tree that kept Cooper's horse secured. The man looked healthy enough and, judging by his well-cut leather clothes, seemed to be far from destitute. The man reached beneath the belly of his horse and released its cinch strap. Cooper watched him drag the saddle from the horse's steaming back and drop it on the opposite side of the campfire.

Cooper pointed to the coffee pot. 'Help yourself, stranger!'

The man nodded. He picked up the solitary tin cup and filled it to its brim. He held the cup in his gloved hands and stared at Cooper through the steam.

'You alone up here?' the stranger asked.

Cooper nodded and pointed with his left hand whilst his right kept a firm grip on his gun. 'Yep! Bin rounding up stray steers and guiding them back to the range over yonder.'

The man turned his head and then sat down. He propped his back against his saddle and looked at the glittering lights of the town below them.

'What's the name of that town?'

Cooper was about to answer when the man spoke again.

'I bin looking for a place called Apache Wells. Is that Apache Wells?'

Cooper shrugged. 'Nope! Apache Wells is a hundred miles south of here.'

'No matter! One town's as good as another!' The stranger lifted the cup to his lips. His icy stare gazed at the man who was easing himself down beside the fire. There was a strange look in the stranger's face. A look which chilled the cowboy. 'Can I have me some of that bacon, pard?'

'Nope!' Cooper answered quickly. 'That's all I got

11

left and I need it more than you!'

The stranger nodded, then looked hard at the gun in the cowboy's hand. 'You gonna put that .44 down?'

Cooper was uneasy. He trusted most men but for some reason had doubts about doing so with the man clad entirely in black.

'You got yourself a pair of mighty fine guns yourself, friend! They looks as though they've bin used a few times!'

'Hell! Don't you trust me?' The man sipped at the strong beverage. 'I could have killed you before I rode out of them trees.'

'I ain't sure if I trust you or not,' Cooper admitted. 'You don't look like most folks I know! You trouble me a tad!'

The stranger lowered his cup until it rested on the edge of the ashes. He let it go and leaned back against the saddle. His eyes were unblinking as they burned through the smoke and licking flames at the cowboy from beneath the hat brim. 'Cautious! I like that in a man! Means you got brains under that hat crown! But think about it a while; you're just a cowpoke and ain't got nothing I want so why be worried about me?'

Dan Cooper thought about the words, then released the hammer of his gun and slid it back into its frayed holster. No sooner had his fingers released their grip on the .44 than he heard something.

It was the sound of the man drawing one of his matched weapons and cocking it in one swift, fluid action. Cooper stared at the barrel of the gleaming weapon. It was aimed straight at his chest. He looked at the stranger. There was a cruel smile etched on the features of the man.

'What you doing, friend?' Cooper asked.

The man did not reply. His trigger finger eased back. A blast of deafening fury exploded from the barrel. Cooper felt the impact of the bullet as it knocked him flat on his back. A fountain of blood gave the only sign that the deadly shot had gone straight into the cowboy's heart. His head rolled to the side as life left him.

The man smiled and twirled his weapon until it went back into its hand-tooled holster. He leaned over the flames and picked up the skillet. His eyes focused on the bacon.

'I lied about you not having something I want, pard,' the stranger told the dead cowboy before picking up a rasher and biting it. 'You had supper and I'm damn hungry!'

ONE

The town was large even by Texan standards. It sat between two tree-clad mountains and bathed beneath a merciless sun which moved mostly through cloudless sky. Beyond, a vast range of fertile grass swayed like the waves of an ocean and seemed to go on for ever. Folks had settled here because of the crystal-clear river that ran down from the nearest of the mountains and fed the range through which it snaked.

To put down roots, all that men with settlers' blood flowing though their veins needed in the West was a plentiful supply of water and salt with a good ration of courage thrown in. Those who had discovered this place knew that if they provided the courage the land itself would provide the rest. So it had been for more than a decade and the town showed no sign of slowing down its steady growth.

Steers grazed on the sweet grass and twice a year they would be rounded up by their owners and sent east to fill the bellies of those who had acquired an appetite for the beef that only this land could supply. Yet like so many other areas of Texas there was hardly any law, and what there was had a very short life-expectancy. To pin a tin star upon one's vest in towns like this was like painting a target on oneself.

But even so, there were men who dared to take that ultimate risk, to try and bring a slim particle of civilization to an otherwise barbarous land.

Narrower streets had spurred off from the original main street as the town grew. Like the legs of a giant spider they spread out in every direction. Now about 200 buildings stood along these streets, yet none was too far from the river.

Although the town appeared to be an Eden, the people who populated it felt that more likely it had been Satan who had really created this land. For it was brutal and full of traps designed to ensnare the unwary. Things had never gone sweetly here. So many souls had perished within the boundaries of the ordinary-looking settlement.

Towns like this were built on the blood of those who had come before. Boot hill stood to the east of the town upon a small rise. Its hundreds of wooden and stone markers bore testament to the fact that places such as this might never truly be accepted into the fabric of civilization.

But men here did not want to be tamed. They had been around long before the law had hung up its shingle and pinned a tin star to the chest of anyone who thought he might be able to tame the unruly two-legged mustangs.

Some mustangs could never be broken.

Never be tamed.

Not one grown man inside the boundaries of the sun-bleached town ever went outdoors without their guns strapped around their hips. They often forgot to place their Stetsons on top of their heads but they never forgot their guns.

Life in the West was already far too short and to be unarmed was tantamount to being suicidal.

Gun law still ruled here.

Even with a town marshal and two deputies on the payroll things still tended to go the way they had always gone. Men were still men in this place.

They lived and died that way.

They liked it that way.

Yet even without the polite Eastern manners that had slowly overtaken so many other Western settlements, things were not quite as wild as the dime novels might have suggested to the gullible readers on the Eastern seaboard. Few men used their weaponry without a reason. Often the reasons were simply the result of bad liquor but they usually had reasons. Men settled their disputes their own way and that way was always with hot lead. Those who knew how to use the gun gathered here in abundance. Some were men wanted in other states and territories, who found that as long as they kept their noses clean they would never be targeted for the bounty money on their heads.

The town had earned its reputation for being brutal, wild and dangerous. It relished the old ways which had served them since the town had first risen out of the wilderness. Men wanted the law like a rancher wanted his herd to get anthrax. But even so the law existed. Backshooters who could not get away with the favourite excuse of 'self-defence' had to be rounded up by someone. That was what the men with tin stars mainly did. That and make sure the gambling houses and saloons did not cheat so many times that it became a problem, and last but not least ensure that the soiled doves of the countless brothels gave value for money and did not cause any trouble between their patrons.

The marshal and his deputies were like referees who stood between bloodied prize-fighters. They vainly attempted to keep the peace whilst most of the less law-abiding citizens did exactly what they wanted to do. When dealing with folks who carried guns you had to be careful and those who had never mastered that art rested up on boot hill.

17

This town remained dangerous.

Maybe that was why none of those who lived within the limits of its sprawling array of buildings had never changed its name.

It still prided itself on that ominous name. A name that was painted in red at all four approaching trails.

This was a town called Death.

TWO

Rufas Kane was a man who had spent more than half of his fifty years hunting the most elusive of prey. Whilst some sought game to sell to those who were incapable of killing, Kane had hunted gold. The fever that was said to be more addictive than opium had captured the soul of the obdurate man long ago when he had accidentally stumbled upon a few nuggets. That had been his downfall for he had wasted the rest of his life vainly attempting to discover more. Now, ragged and weatherworn and looking far older than his true age, Kane seldom ventured down from the mountainside unless he was short of provisions. He spent his time moving through the forested slopes looking for anything that resembled the precious ore he craved.

With only his mule for company Kane tended to keep away from people, who had a habit of mocking him. So it had been by sheer accident, as he descended through the trees towards the still smoking campfire that he saw the nervous quarter horse still tethered to the tree where Dan Cooper had secured it.

At first Kane was about to turn around and seek another way down to the valley. Then he spotted the cowboy's body sprawled out on the ground. Kane was not a curious man by nature but the sight had intrigued him. The sun had risen two hours earlier and he knew that most cowboys rose with the light of a new day.

So why was this cowboy still lying there?

Kane led his mule slowly down the steep slope and muttered to himself as all loners do. The rays of the sun bathed the hillside in its glorious light and gave an answer to the man's questions.

The blood had already dried but there was no mistaking the fact that the cowboy had been murdered. Kane held his mule in check as it shied away from the sickly scent of death which hung over the campsite. Kane stopped when he reached the horse and looked at it for a long time before he looped his own reins around the girth of the tree trunk and knotted the leathers.

Even men who spent most of their lives high in the vast wilderness could be shocked by the image of merciless murder and Kane was no exception. He rubbed his long bearded chin and forced himself to walk closer to the corpse. Kane's eyes screwed up as he stared down at the evidence of a brutal slaying.

He had seen many men killed but this seemed strangely different to Kane. Walking around the scene he swung his thin arms wildly at the feasting flies. He then looked at the still smoking ashes and the skillet which had a hole burned through its pan. The coffee pot had not fared much better. It was all confusing to Kane. He paused for a moment, then his gaze shifted to the ground opposite to where the cowboy's festering body lay. It was clear that someone else had also bedded down here, he thought.

Someone who had fired his gun across the fire and killed the cowboy.

Boot-tracks led away from the killing.

For the first time since Kane had discovered the body he felt nervous. Real nervous. His head swung around as his eyes looked for the killer who, he knew, could not be far away. Kane swallowed hard when he realized that the ruthless killer who had done this might do exactly the same to him.

As fast as his thin legs could carry him, Rufas Kane moved back to his mule and pulled his reins free of the tree. Sweat ran down his face as fear overwhelmed him.

'Gotta go tell the marshal!' Kane muttered to himself as he headed down towards the town far

21

below. That had been three hours earlier and the man who hunted gold was still as nervous as he led the marshal and two deputies back to the gruesome scene.

Marshal Don Harper was probably no younger than the man who led the mule but he sure looked younger. Sleeping under the stars in constant battle with the elements had a way of taking the oil out of a man's body as well as the spirit from his soul. The lawman sat astride his gelded bay until he too saw the sight at the edge of the tree line. He drew back on his reins and signalled his two deputies to do the same.

All three law officers dismounted. Ben Jones was the older of the deputies and had been with the marshal for two years. He took the reins from Harper and then turned to the eighteen-year-old Clevis Tork.

'Stay here with the horses, Clevis.'

The youngster nodded. He had no desire to venture any closer to the body. He watched as the three men waded through the buzzing swarms of flies.

Harper rested one set of knuckles on his gun grip as the fingers of his other hand stroked his chin. He had listened to Kane's rantings all the way up the side of the mountain and now realized that every word was true.

'Ain't this Coop, Ben?' the marshal asked his deputy.

Jones nodded slowly. 'Reckon so. That's Coop's quarter horse and no mistakes. Ain't never seen his face twisted up like that before though. Looks like he was staring straight into the face of the Devil just before he was shot!'

Harper edged around the body and then looked to where Kane was pointing at the marks on the ground.

'I figure someone slept there, Marshal,' Kane stammered.

'Someone was bedded down here right enough, Rufas,' Harper said as he knelt closer to the churned-up ground. 'Whoever it was must have just gunned Coop. Killed him like a dog!'

Jones moved around the mule and bent over. 'Coop's gun is in his holster, Don.'

'So it weren't no showdown over a confab that got out of hand,' the marshal surmised as he straightened back up. 'Whoever was bedded down this side of the fire just shot Coop. Why? Coop was a likeable cowpoke who would never have caused no one any trouble.'

Jones walked to the quarter horse. His eyes looked down at the ground and then he saw the hoof-tracks on the opposite side of the tree trunk.

'I got me some tracks here, Don! Ain't Coop's horse. Must belong to the killer's mount.'

The marshal walked quickly to where his deputy

was standing and then looked down at the hoof-marks. 'You're right, Ben! Coop's horse couldn't have gotten around this side of the tree.'

Jones rested a hand on the trunk of the tree and stared hard at the tracks. He shook his head, then looked at the marshal.

'Ain't no way we could tell them shoe-marks from any other horse in these parts, Don.'

'Yeah! I noticed that. Just brand-new shoes straight off a blacksmith's forge!' Harper sighed. 'Identical to almost every other set.'

Kane moved closer to the two lawmen. 'Why'd anyone shoot a cowboy, Marshal?'

Harper bit his lip. 'No sane man would have, Rufas.'

'You mean this killer is loco, Don?' Jones asked.

'Or just a snivelling coward who likes to kill folks with their guns holstered, Ben.'

Kane moved even closer to the two lawmen. 'You figure he's still up here? I'm a tad scared!'

'Ain't no call to be scared, Rufas,' Jones told him. 'He's probably high-tailed it by now.'

'I don't think so, boys,' Harper disagreed.

Jones stepped closer to his marshal. 'What you mean, Ben?'

Harper rubbed the corners of his dry mouth with the tails of his bandanna and squinted hard down at the town below them.

'Nope! This killer ain't the sort to high-tail it. I reckon that bastard is down there now. Down in Death! Maybe he's even looking for his next easy kill!'

Jones went ashen and waved to Tork. 'Git over here and help us heave this body over his horse, Clevis.'

Harper spat at the ground. 'We've gotta get him before he dips his fingers in blood again, boys.'

THREE

Death was busy. The sun had brought out most of the men, women and children as it always did. The sound of the school bell echoed around the wooden buildings as one store after another opened their doors to greet those who went about their daily rituals. The smell of fresh-baked bread filled Main Street as the bakers opened up to sell their wares. Buckboards moved in every direction as the first of the day's stagecoaches was readied outside the Wells Fargo depot. At least 200 souls moved in every direction. Most were on foot, some were mounted. Death and those who lived there had no call to think that this was to be anything but another day cast in the same mould as so many others that had gone before it.

But this day was to be different.

Very different.

The horseman clad in black leather who had ridden in just after sunup had seemed to melt into the very fabric of the unruly town. He had looped his reins to the hitching rail outside the town's only hotel, rented a room for the week and then walked the 200 yards to the nearest of the numerous drinking holes. The Red Branch saloon was like all the others. Riddled with bullet holes and requiring a coat of paint it stood awaiting another day of boisterous trade. For Death had many thirsty citizens and the few hours during which saloons closed each morning was barely enough time to empty the spittoons and put fresh sawdust down.

The twisted features of the stranger with the matched pair of Colts strapped to his hips should have warned the weary that this was no normal soul. The cruel smile should have told them that this was a man who valued nothing except his own life.

Trey Skinner had walked across the empty saloon towards the baggy-eyed bartender with the expression of a man who had not even seen hard liquor for months. He licked his lips and placed a gloved hand on the wet bar counter. He stared at the array of bottles spread out in front of the long mottled mirror behind the bartender, who sported a long black moustache.

'What'll it be?'

Skinner rubbed his chin as his eyes darted from

one bottle to the next. He continued to smile as though something inside his twisted brain kept telling him jokes no one else could either hear or understand.

'That bottle with the unbroken seal!' Skinner pointed.

The bartender pointed. 'This 'un?'

Skinner nodded. 'Yep!'

'This is real fine whiskey, mister!' the bartender said. 'It costs twenty bucks a bottle! You sure you got enough?'

The face of the ruthless killer suddenly altered expression as the words of the man with the white apron strapped around his waist sank in.

'You saying that I don't look like I can afford good whiskey, barkeep? That what you're saying?'

Joe White had been the main bartender of the Red Branch since the saloon had been erected. He had seen many men over the years but suddenly he realized that this one was different. The fancy clothes belied the fact that they encased a man with bad blood flowing through his veins.

'I-I ain't trying to rile you none, stranger. I just didn't want you to think I was robbing you. This is imported from San Francisco. Only a few of the richer folks in town favour it.'

'Git that bottle and place it here.' Skinner pointed at the counter before him as he dragged a thimble-glass from a stack of fresh-washed ones. He turned the glass over and ran a gloved finger over its rim.

White did as he was told. He placed the bottle down, then stepped back. He watched as the stranger tore the seal off the cork and placed it between his blackened teeth. He pulled the cork and spat it away. Another customer entered the Red Branch and ambled up to the bar. He said nothing as he watched the bartender and Skinner eyeing each other up.

'That's twenty bucks,' White said in a faltering tone.

Skinner did not respond. He poured the amber liquor into the glass then raised it to his lips. He inhaled its fumes, then he downed the whiskey in one throw. It burned like a forest fire as it made its way down into his guts.

'Good whiskey, barkeep,' he muttered. 'Damn good!'

White held out his hand and repeated. 'Twenty bucks.'

The smile returned to Skinner's face as he refilled the glass and repeated the swift, satisfying action. He sighed and stared hard at the bartender.

'Twenty dollars? You want I should pay you?'

Nervously, White nodded. 'Yep.'

'I've killed men for less than twenty bucks.' Skinner said as he again filled his glass and downed its contents. 'That make you scared?'

'Yep.' White replied honestly.

The gunman poked a finger and thumb into his vest pocket and pulled out a few coins. He tossed them at the man, then grabbed both bottle and glass.

'Just recall that I didn't gun you down,' Skinner said with a smile.

'Yes, sir!'

The deadly gunman looked around the room and saw a chair with its back up against the wall close to the window. 'I'm gonna go sit by the window yonder, barkeep! Sit by the window and drink this whiskey! That OK by you?'

Joe White slowly nodded. 'Yep.'

More than three hours had passed but every second within the smoke-filled drinking place had felt like an eternity to its nervous patrons.

The whiskey bottle was nearly empty as the white-faced wall clock chimed one in the afternoon, Trey Skinner was still sitting in the Red Branch, close to the window. His eyes narrowed when he saw the marshal and his two deputies riding back into town leading the quarter horse with Cooper's body tied across its saddle. Skinner stood, lifted the bottle and finished its contents. He watched through the cracked window panes as the lawmen headed up to the undertaker's parlour. The saloon was now half-full but eerily quiet. Only when the smiling man dressed in black leather walked back out into the sun-baked street did their voices suddenly rise.

FOUR

The streetlights of Death glowed their amber illumination across the twisting streets as the five horsemen guided their dust-caked mounts along Main Street towards the brightest of all the saloons' façades. Rancher Gene Adams drew rein first and stopped his tall chestnut mare in front of one of the hitching rails. He sat in his saddle for a few moments, studying the town and those who filled its streets. He said nothing as his cowboys lined up beside him on their tired horses. There was a smell which lingered in towns like Death and it was not an odour favoured by the silver-haired rancher. He preferred the fresh air of his ranch far to the west, not the stench that all towns seemed to create. Men drank too much and pleasured themselves too often in towns like Death and that had never been his way. The hard-working rancher rose in his saddle, then slowly dismounted.

He looped and tied his reins before stooping under the weathered pole and stepping up on to the boardwalk.

Adams watched as his men slowly copied his actions. His oldest friend, the wily Tomahawk, had not stopped grumbling since they had ridden from their ranch more than a week earlier and even the promise of free whiskey could not seem to stop the bearded old-timer from constantly complaining.

Johnny Puma knotted his reins to the pole and patted his pinto pony before hopping over the twisted wooden shaft and joining the tall rancher.

Top wrangler Kelso Scott sucked on what was left of his cigarette and carefully lowered his lean body down on to the dusty street. He waited for the youngest member of their outfit, Clu Brooks to drop to the ground before he too secured his reins and stepped up outside the busy saloon. Unlike the other cowboys Brooks had never been to Death before; he seemed nervous. This was a rowdy place and the eighteen-year-old kept close to the older Scott.

Adams inhaled the stale air and shook his head. 'This town is starting to smell like its name, boys!'

All four of his cowboys nodded in agreement.

'They oughta dig themselves some new outhouses or buy some lime, Gene boy,' Tomahawk said, staring into the window of the saloon.

Adams looked at the swing doors and then over

them. The interior of the Broken Bottle was well lit by numerous coal-tar lanterns but the fug of cigar and pipe smoke made it virtually impossible to see as far as the bar counter. But the bar girls could be seen as they gathered close to the doors at the approach of the strangers in town.

Tomahawk held out a hand to the rancher. 'C'mon, Gene! You said we was gonna have us a good drink on you and I ain't gonna let you wriggle out of that deal!'

The rancher reached inside his coat pocket and pulled out a half golden eagle and looked at it for a while. He knew that there would not be any change once his boys began to quench their thirst.

'If I'd not needed you all to help me with buying us a herd of horseflesh I could have saved myself a pretty penny,' he mused.

A skinny old hand shook under the rancher's nose as Tomahawk squinted up at Adams.

'Come on! I'm dying of thirst here, boy! I ain't getting any younger, either!'

Adams smiled, then turned to Johnny and gave him the shining coin. 'Don't let this old coot drink nothing stronger than beer, Johnny. Don't let none of them drink nothing stronger than beer. If I smell whiskey on any of you I'll dock you a month's pay. Savvy?'

Johnny closed his gloved hand around the coin.

'Beer is fine with me, Gene.'

Tomahawk was still grumbling as the four cowboys entered the smoky saloon. Gene Adams rubbed his neck and glanced across at the marshal's office directly opposite. He headed for it. The lights from the office made a bright outline round the ill-fitting window blinds.

The street was busy. Riders were still moving up and down its length as men searched for things they knew could be found anywhere in this wild place. The only difference was that if you looked hard enough you just might be able to find your pleasure a little more cheaply.

Adams stepped up on to the boardwalk, turned the brass doorknob and entered the office. Three men were sitting around the office. Each of them looked up at the familiar face, which smiled at them in return.

'As I live and breathe, if it ain't old Gene Adams!' Marshal Don Harper said with a surprised tone in his voice. 'I ain't seen you in a month of Sundays! What brings you this far east?'

'Horses!' Adams said, resting his hip on the edge of the desk. 'I need me fifty or more head of horseflesh and I can't seem to find any in all of Texas.'

'There's a good reason for that, Gene,' Harper said.

'And that is?'

'The army bin buying hundreds of the things to send north for the cavalry.' Harper pulled his pipe from his vest pocket and sucked on it a while before opening his tobacco pouch. 'I heard me a rumour they're building a hundred forts on the Plains to keep the Cheyenne and Sioux knuckled down.'

Adams scratched his jaw thoughtfully. 'Damn it all! I need at least fifty head for my next trail-drive to McCoy. I got two thousand longhorns to get to the railhead there. Can't set out without a damn big remuda of horses.'

Harper placed his pipe-stem between his teeth, struck a match and lit the well-primed bowl. He puffed a few times, then tossed the match aside.

'I thought you had plenty of horses?'

'Did have,' Adams said with a sigh. 'Until some rustlers helped themselves to my second string on the lower pastures. Reckon they headed them south to the border. We'd have followed but there ain't the time. I have to get the cattle drive started before the end of the month or we'll not have enough grazing for the beef on the trail north.'

Harper removed his pipe and pointed it at the rancher. 'I think Barney Drew has a lot of horses. Most of them ain't bin broke but he's got a lot of them.'

'Drew of the Circle D?'

The marshal nodded. 'Yep. Just south of town.'

Adams stood up. 'As I recall, he sells mighty sound animals, Don!'

'Best around!' Harper agreed. 'He travels miles looking for wild herds and cuts out the best to sell to anyone who got the money to meet his price.'

'Is his price high?' Adams wondered aloud.

'Damn high!' Harper grinned. 'And getting higher the more the army buys. You'll probably have to pay as much as twenty bucks a head. Maybe even more.'

Adams nodded and turned back for the door. He paused, then looked at the man with the gleaming tin star on his vest.

'My boys are over in the Broken Bottle washing the trail dust out of their mouths. Reckon they'll be there for another hour or so. Do you want to come down to the café and share a few lies over a couple of steaks?'

Harper rose quickly. 'You paying?'

'Damn right!' Adams patted his friend on the back and led him back to the door. 'You know I never miss a chance to bribe a lawman.'

Deputies Tork and Jones watched enviously as the two older men left the office. They looked at the clock on the wall.

'Ain't even seven yet, Clevis,' Jones said with a sigh. He rubbed his grumbling belly.

'When do we get to eat, Ben?' Tork asked.

'When Don comes back.'

'When do you figure that will be?'

Ben Jones got to his feet. He walked to the steaming coffee pot on top of the stove and lifted it. It was heavy. He glanced at the younger man.

'This is full and I figure we got us time to drink it all before those two quit eating.'

FIVE

The Broken Bottle was almost overflowing. The four cowboys had managed to find themselves a place at the far end of the long bar counter and were supping on their umpteenth beer. A fluttering set of eyelashes had caused Scott to trail one of the smiling bar girls up to the landing.

'We ain't gonna see him for a while,' Johnny Puma observed with a wry grin on his face.

Clu Brooks held his beer-glass and filled the place left vacant by the wrangler. 'Where's Kelso going with that female, Johnny?'

Both Tomahawk and Johnny stared into their drinks and tried not to show their amusement by the innocent cowboy's question.

'Didn't you know that's his aunt, Clu?' Tomahawk lied.

Brooks raised an eyebrow. 'She's awful young to be

his aunt, Tomahawk.'

'That's just face-paint, boy,' Tomahawk assured him.

'It is?'

Johnny rested a hand on the shoulders of the curious cowboy and smiled. 'Look around. All these females are covered in face-paint, Clu.'

'They are?' Brooks cast his eyes on all the other women in the saloon. 'Yeah! Now you mention it they are all kinda bright-cheeked and no mistake.'

'Apaches don't paint themselves up that much,' Johnny grinned.

'Some of them women are older than me!' Tomahawk managed to say without laughing.

Brooks returned his attention to the landing where Scott had just disappeared into a room with the bar girl.

'What they gonna do up there?'

'Talk,' Johnny said firmly.

Brooks shrugged and looked around the room again. A half-dozen tables were filled with men playing poker whilst the others remained occupied by those who preferred to just drink. To his left in the shadows such as only a corner can create a man clad entirely in black leather sat with an empty bottle of whiskey before him. The ruthless Trey Skinner had his next victim already picked out.

Just as Brooks was about to ask another of his

painfully naïve questions, a man in a handsome tailored suit moved up to the counter and looked all three cowboys up and down. The man's paunch was held in by a red silk vest covered in silver buttons. He touched the brim of his hat and smiled.

'Do any of you gentlemen partake in the noble art of poker?' he asked.

Johnny and Tomahawk turned and faced the man. They eyed him from his polished shoes to his well-brushed hat. He was impressive in these parts. It was also obvious that he did not toil to earn his living.

'We do sometimes,' Johnny replied.

'If'n the game's straight!' Tomahawk added.

'Would you care to sit in?' The man gestured to a table across the room where one man sat shuffling a deck of well-thumbed cards. 'My friend and I have been quite fortunate this evening but our opponents have quit! Would you care to sit in and try your luck?'

'You fleeced them,' Tomahawk said.

'My associate and myself are honest gamblers, sir.' The man smiled. 'We just happen to be good poker-players.'

Johnny looked at the money in his hand and then at Tomahawk, who was nodding in his direction.

'Sure. Me and Tomahawk will try a few hands with you.'

The man looked at Brooks. 'What about you, my young friend?'

41

Tomahawk stepped between them. 'Clu don't know nothing about games of chance, mister! Leave him to prop up the bar! It would take an hour or more just to explain the rules to him!'

The man smiled again. 'I understand!'

Johnny handed a silver dollar to the young cowboy. 'This'll keep you in beer 'til me and Tomahawk get back with our winnings, Clu!'

Brooks nodded. He slipped the coin into his pants pocket and leaned on the bar counter. He could see his friends sitting down at the table in the reflection of the saloon mirror.

The departure of the two older and wiser cowhands was all the reason Skinner required to rise from his chair and move in on the quiet Brooks.

'That all you drink, boy?' a voice asked from the darkened corner along the bar. 'Beer? That's a woman's drink in these parts, ya'know?'

Brooks turned his head and stared at the man who held a whiskey bottle in one hand and a glass in the other. He straightened up as the man moved towards him.

'Was you talking to me?' Brooks asked.

Trey Skinner placed the bottle down on the wet surface of the counter and finished what was left in his glass.

'Yep! I was talking to you.'

Brooks looked the man up and down. He had

never seen anyone clad entirely in black leather before. The hand-tooled gunbelt with its gleaming matched Colts was also something he seldom saw. Whatever this stranger was it was certain that he was no cowboy, he thought.

'I like beer.'

'Men drink whiskey, boy.'

Brooks glanced across at his two friends. They had not seen the man close in on him and he felt a trifle anxious. He cleared his throat and tried to change the subject.

'Them guns are mighty fancy, mister,' he remarked, patting his own holstered gun which showed signs of rust. 'I never had me no call to use a gun.'

'What you wearing one for then?' Skinner asked.

'We all gotta wear one in case we have to use it,' Brooks replied drily. 'Sometimes horses break their legs and gotta be shot.'

'These are the best guns in all of Texas,' Skinner bragged. 'The best guns for the best gunman!'

Brooks swallowed hard. 'Gunman? You're a real gunman?'

'Yep!' Skinner nodded hard. 'What you think I was, boy? A baker?'

'I ain't never met me a real live gunman before.' Brooks could not help the sound of admiration in his youthful voice.

43

Skinner edged closer. He slid both bottle and glass along with him.

'How come you're drinking beer, kid? You a man or just a wet-behind-the-ears boy?'

Brooks felt insulted. He stretched up to his full height and tried to expand his chest.

'I'm a man, OK! Don't you go calling me names.'

'You're a man? That's to be seen.' Skinner lifted the bottle and filled his glass before pouring some of his whiskey into the beer glass.

Brooks was open-mouthed. His eyes looked down at his drink and then back at the man who was now no more than arm's length from him.

'I ain't meant to drink whiskey!' the cowboy exclaimed.

A cruel smile lit up Skinner's face.

'You ain't allowed? Somebody gonna spank you?'

'No, sir! There ain't nobody gonna spank me.'

Skinner swilled down his own whiskey. 'You gotta drink like a man if you want folks to think you are one, boy!'

Brooks swallowed hard again. His eyes looked up at the mirror behind the bartender. Tomahawk and Johnny were now deeply engrossed in their poker game and totally oblivious to anything else. He then gazed towards the door on the landing where Scott had gone. Then he looked back at Skinner.

'I'm a man! I don't need no hard liquor to prove it!'

The gunman nodded. 'Tell me. Who don't allow you to drink whiskey? Your ma? Your pa? Who likes you to stay a snot-nosed little boy?'

Brooks felt angry. 'Mr Adams. He gave us orders not to drink nothing stronger than beer coz we have to work tomorrow rounding up a heap of mustangs.'

'Who is Mr Adams?'

'My boss,' Brooks told him. 'He's mighty tough on us if we drink hard liquor.'

Skinner's smile grew wider. 'You're a coward, boy! No backbone at all in that body of yours, is there? Letting folks order you around!'

Brooks felt hot. His manhood had been questioned. He loosened his bandanna and grabbed at the glass. He raised it to his lips and downed the contents in one throw. He placed the glass down and dried his mouth on his sleeve.

'Satisfied?'

Skinner lifted the bottle again and poured another three fingers of his whiskey into the cowboy's beer-glass. This time there was no beer to dilute its strength. He smiled and pushed it to the hands of the cowboy.

'I will be if you drink that as well, boy!'

With furrowed brow, Brooks leaned forward until their noses were almost touching. 'Will you quit calling me a boy then? I'm getting a tad annoyed!'

'Drink that and I might just figure I was wrong,'

45

Skinner sneered at his chosen prey.

'OK!' Brooks lifted his glass and swallowed the whiskey in one gulp. His eyes began to glisten as the powerful liquor burned its way down his throat. He placed his glass back down and coughed. 'Now will you leave me be?'

Trey Skinner tilted his head. 'You telling me to go someplace, boy?'

'Yep!' Brooks nodded. 'Away! Go away!'

'Or what?'

'Or I'll get real ornery.' Brooks waved a finger at the deadly gunman. 'I've just about had my fill with you!'

'You threatening me, kid?'

Brooks inhaled deeply. 'I sure am.'

'I don't like the tone in your voice,' Skinner said loud enough to drag every eye in the Broken Bottle to him. He poked a finger into the chest of the young cowboy. 'You don't own this saloon. I'll drink wherever I damn well likes!'

Suddenly the men and women close to the bar saw the two men and knew what was about to happen. They all began to move away.

The gloved finger had hurt. Brooks rubbed his chest and gritted his teeth.

'I don't care what you like, just leave me alone!'

Skinner slapped Brooks's face as hard as he could. The young cowhand staggered, then lowered his head. A fury fuelled by the unfamiliar whiskey now swept over him. He clenched a fist and swung it at Skinner. The deadly gunman blocked the punch and then slapped Brooks even harder. The empty beer-glass went flying off the counter and smashed into a million fragments.

'Just a little boy trying to be a man,' Skinner said, laughing; then he whispered just loud enough for only one man to be able to hear his mocking words, 'But then all cowboys are a little bit different from real men, ain't they? Maybe you ain't a boy after all! Maybe you're a girl! Are you? Are you?'

'You dirt-mouthed bastard!' Brooks yelled out.

Tomahawk and Johnny were about to rise from the card table when to their horror they saw their young pal reach for his gun and draw.

'No!' Johnny yelled out across the saloon.

It was too late.

Skinner had waited for Brooks's weapon to clear its holster, then he drew one of his own pristine guns. He fired once. Once was enough to send the cowboy spinning on his heels before crashing down into the stale sawdust.

Johnny Puma had ploughed through the tables, people and chairs but it had been in vain. No man could run as fast as a bullet could travel. The cowboy stopped and stared down at the youngster. Clu Brooks lay in a pool of blood staring up with lifeless eyes at the man who had just killed him.

It was as though every female in the saloon had screamed at exactly the same moment. The chilling sound rang around the interior of the Broken Bottle.

Then, above them, a door was opened. A half-dressed Kelso Scott ran out on to the landing. He looked down in utter shock. Johnny turned his head and stared through the gunsmoke at Skinner. Then he flexed his own fingers above his gungrips.

'You killed Clu!' Johnny raged.

Tomahawk grabbed his friend in a bear hug and dragged him back. 'No, Johnny! No!'

Johnny lowered his head and stared at the man with the twisted smile carved across his face. It was a sight that no man could ever forget once he had seen it.

'Let me go, Tomahawk! I got me some killing to do!'

'No, boy!' the old-timer shouted as his thin arms managed to hold the younger man in check. Scott ran down the staircase and skidded to a halt when his eyes saw the youngster. The wrangler rested an arm on the bar and said nothing.

The smoking Colt was still in Skinner's hand when the saloon swing doors burst apart. Everyone inside the Broken Bottle looked at the marshal and Gene Adams as they rushed into the saloon with their own guns drawn. Within the beat of a racing heart the pair of deputies had joined them.

Harper looked at his men. 'Don't let nobody leave here 'til I tells you.'

'You bet!' Ben Jones nodded.

The two older men headed towards the gruesome scene.

Adams's eyes narrowed as they focused upon the dead cowboy on the floor in front of them. 'Sweet Lord! Not him!'

'Nobody move!' Harper shouted at the crowd. He paused when he reached the bar. He looked down at the dead Brooks. The bloodstained shirt with the small blackened bullet hole at its centre was sickening even to his experienced eyes.

Adams dropped on to one knee and pressed his fingers against Brooks's neck. There was no pulse. He then shook his head and closed the eyelids of the dead man. Adams rose again and silently glared at Skinner.

'He was one of my boys, mister!' Adams rasped.

'Self-defence!' Skinner spat.

Harper moved closer and pointed his own .45 at the one in the gunman's hand.

'Holster that hogleg,' he growled.

Skinner shrugged and obeyed. 'He started it, Marshal. Ask anyone who drew first. I was just defending myself.'

'Is that right?' Harper shouted at the people who

49

fringed the saloon walls. 'Did the kid draw first?'

A half-dozen people nodded.

Harper returned his icy glare at the gunman. 'What's your name, mister?'

'Trey Skinner.'

'Never heard of you.'

Johnny managed to free himself from the arms of Tomahawk. He pointed a finger at the remorseless Skinner. 'You must have riled him up, stranger. That boy wouldn't have harmed a fly. What you say to him? How'd you get him so all-fired up?'

Skinner leaned against the bar. 'Nothing! The kid was drunk and started to yell at me coz I wouldn't give him any of my rye. I slapped him and he went for his gun.'

'That boy never even fired his gun before,' Johnny snarled.

'Maybe he thought he could become famous like Billy the Kid,' Skinner suggested. 'He started the play and I just finished it. Self-defence. Ain't no law against a man defending his life.'

Adams pushed his way through the crowd until he was standing within a whisker of the gunman.

'I don't know how or why you did this, mister, but I'm telling you something and you better heed my words. If I find out that you killed that boy in cold blood I'll kill you.'

Skinner smiled. 'I'm trembling, old man.'

'You ought to be,' Adams told him grimly. 'I don't need to hide behind the law when I decide vermin needs killing.'

Johnny faced Adams. 'Let me take this varmint out into the street and have a showdown, Gene. I'll make him pay.'

Adams dismissed the words. 'You quit that kinda talk right now, Johnny.'

Trey Skinner poured himself another whiskey and smiled as he downed it. 'Listen to the old man! He might just be saving you from ending up like the kid.'

Adams turned and powerfully ushered his men to where Brooks lay. Scott looked at the rancher and nodded.

'Me and Johnny will get Clu out of here, Gene.'

Adams looked at Johnny. 'You heard Kelso, son. Pick Clu up and take him to the undertaker's.'

Marshal Harper rested a hand on Adams's shoulder. 'I'll show you where the undertaker's parlour is, Gene.'

'Much obliged, Don.' Adams nodded his thanks.

Scott and Johnny lifted Brooks off the floor and carried him towards the swing doors. With the dead cowboy's hat in his thin hands, Tomahawk walked a few paces behind them pensively as Harper and Adams trailed the downcast group. The street was cool but the tall rancher did not notice. As they reached the boardwalk he looked back over the doors into the Broken Bottle and at the man who was still smiling.

'I'm sorry, Gene,' Harper said.

'Weren't your fault, Don.'

'It feels as though it was though.'

'Who is this Skinner *hombre*, Don?'

'I ain't never set eyes on him before, Gene.'

'I reckon we'll see a lot more of him before long.' Adams rested his hands on top of his gungrips and continued to walk after his men in the direction of the undertaker's.

The closer they got to their goal the more the marshal started to think about the other dead cowboy whom he and his deputies had retrieved from the mountainside earlier that day. Dan Cooper had been killed with one deadly accurate shot too. He rubbed his neck and wondered.

'What's wrong, Don?' Adams asked.

'I ain't too sure, Gene,' the seasoned lawman replied thoughtfully as they trailed the cowboys carrying their sorrowful burden.

SIX

An hour had passed and yet it felt no more than a mere heartbeat to the two men inside the building, which had seen more than its fair share of trade during the previous decade. The showy velvet drapes that hung in the office could not disguise what lay beyond in the rear room. Those whose business was dealing with death could never truly veil the horrible reality of their occupation no matter how hard they tried. When folks died it took a certain breed of man to handle the hideous actuality. No matter how much they sugared the pill it still had a taste that nobody wished to savour. The undertaker had washed both bodies and laid them out on two tables at the rear of his parlour. Both dead men wore the same stunned expression and similar lethal wounds. As Marshal Harper studied the chests of the two dead cowboys, Adams looked away. The rancher could not take his eyes off the hastily constructed coffins which were stacked against the back wall of the room close to a door which led to the alley. Harper rubbed his chin thoughtfully, then raised an arm and patted the tall rancher's shoulder.

'Look at this, Gene,' he said.

Adams inhaled deeply and turned to where the lawman was pointing. His dark eyebrows rose when he saw what Harper was indicating. He moved closer and rested both his gloved hands on the edge of the closest table.

Two almost identical bullet holes. One in each chest. The holes had both gone in an inch away from the middle of the cowboys' chests. It took a mighty fine shot to destroy a beating heart with only one bullet.

'What you reckon, Gene?'

'Reckon that is a tad strange, Don,' Adams muttered. 'Two dead cowpokes killed with the same heart shot. Can't be an inch difference in them.'

Harper nodded in silent agreement.

'I don't believe in coincidences, Gene. If I was a betting man I'd wager that both your boy and old Coop here were killed by the same man.'

'Skinner!' Adams mumbled the name as though it were tainted with poison. 'You figure that Skinner not only killed my boy but this old cowhand?'

'Yep.' Harper led Adams out into the sumptuously

54

draped front office of the undertaker and leaned on the brass window-rod. He stared at the pair of deputies outside and the three silent cowboys. He looked over his shoulder. 'But knowing and proving are two very different things, *amigo*!'

Adams saw the undertaker close the drapes behind him as he continued to ready the corpses for their final journey up to boot hill. He walked by the lawman's side, removed his black ten-gallon hat and wiped his brow along his coat sleeve.

'Who was this Coop, Don?'

'Just an old cowboy who made his living rounding up steers off the mountainside and heading them back down towards the range, Gene. Most of the folks who own them steers paid him a few bucks a month to ensure they didn't lose too many head. We found him this morning up on the side of the mountain by his campfire. Someone had gunned him down.'

'And he was just shot?' Adams could not understand why even a lowlife like Skinner would kill a poor cowboy. There was no profit in it. 'Not robbed or anything? Just shot!'

'Yep.' Harper sighed. 'Somebody just killed him. Left him on his bedroll for buzzard bait. Whoever it was that done this was bedded down by the signs, Gene. He must have rode in and shared the fire but then drew his gun and blasted old Coop into eternity.'

'Why would anyone do that?'

'Good question, old friend.'

Adams swallowed hard. 'And you ain't never seen this Skinner critter before, Don?'

'Nope.'

'And he's out there walking free to kill anyone else he takes a hankering to.' Adams sighed heavily. 'Somehow he managed to rile up young Clu and get the wet-eared boy to draw first. That means he can hide behind the excuse that it was simply self-defence and not cold-blooded murder!'

'Unlike your boy's, Coop's gun was still in its holster, Gene,' Harper said with a shrug.

Adams returned his hat to his head. 'There weren't no witness up on the mountainside. Skinner could just do his killing whenever it suited him.'

Harper straightened up as a thought came to him. 'Hell! I wonder if'n there's paper on him, Gene? I might have me a poster in the office with his handle on it. If he's wanted someplace I can arrest the bastard.'

'Then let's go take us a look.' The rancher turned the doorknob and pulled the door open.

Both men walked out into the crisp night air. The sounds of the saloons filled their ears as they stood amid their men. Even lethal gunplay could not stop the people of Death from enjoying themselves. But there were those who could not even imagine relishing the numerous pleasures a town like this had to offer.

Adams looked at the faces of Tomahawk, Johnny and Scott. They were still brooding, as all men did when trying to cope with the loss of one of their own. The rancher knew that any one of them might draw his own gun if he even set eyes upon the man who had so brutally killed the young Clu Brooks. If there was revenge to be had, Adams silently vowed that he would be the one to dish it out. He turned.

'Tomahawk!' Adams said firmly.

The old-timer moved towards him, his wrinkled eyes screwed up.

'What you want, Gene boy?'

Adams placed a hand on his bony shoulder and led him just out of range of the others' hearing. He leaned down and whispered into the aged cowboy's ear.

'Reckon you ought to take the boys over to the livery and get the horses bedded down for the night, old-timer,' Adams said.

'Then can we git us a room at the hotel?' asked Tomahawk.

'Nope!' Adams leaned even closer. 'I figure that Skinner has himself a room there. I don't want Johnny or Kelso to brush up against him! I want you to take our bedrolls and pitch them up in the hayloft in the livery. Savvy?'

Tomahawk looked hard at the rancher. 'But if them boys did bump into that Skinner critter I reckon he'd be the one to come off worst.'

'Maybe, but I ain't taking the risk.' Adams sighed, 'I don't wanna lose any more of my boys. Them young 'uns got their dander up and that seems to be what Skinner likes. His kind knows that folks with their souls on fire ain't as good with their guns as men who are calm.'

Tomahawk nodded and scratched his jutting beard. 'Yeah. I see what you mean, boy. Don't go fretting none, I'll spin the boys a yarn about you worrying that someone might steal our horses.'

Adams smiled. 'And if anyone can spin a yarn, it's you.'

'We all gonna bed down in the livery?'

'Yep! We'll all bed down in the loft at the livery.'

The wily old man winked. 'Leave it to me, Gene boy.'

Adams tugged at the white beard. 'I'm relying on you to make sure Johnny and Kelso keep their noses clean.'

Tomahawk shuffled over to the younger cowboys and herded them towards their horses along the street. 'C'mon, you young whippersnappers!'

Kelso and Johnny did as they were told and reluctantly left Adams standing beside the marshal and his deputies.

'Let's go take a look at them Wanted posters of yours, Don,' suggested Adams. The four men crossed the street and headed for the dimly illuminated office.

Adams was thinking that if he kept his cowboys away from the gunman who had slain the youngest of their small band he was protecting them. He had not even considered that Skinner might seek them out no matter where they went. As Tomahawk and his two fellow cowboys unhitched their five horses and started along the dusty street for the livery stables, none of them noticed the shadowy figure who watched their every move.

The murderous Trey Skinner leaned against a wall in an alleyway beside the Broken Bottle and sucked on a cigar. Its smoke drifted over the killer. His eyes burned through the darkness at the men as they led their horses into a side-street.

He had already decided that they deserved a closer look in case he wanted to add them to the well-notched wooden gungrips that he sported on each hip.

Skinner blew out a plume of smoke, then dropped the cigar and crushed it with his left boot into the sand. He eased both his guns in their holsters until he was certain that they were ready for action.

He began to move after them like a wild beast in pursuit of its prey. Every stride of his long legs brought him closer and closer to the cowboys who were leading the string of well-trained horses towards the big stable building that stood at the edge of the sprawling settlement.

Although the streets of Death were filled with men he went unnoticed by any of them. Like a rat, Skinner had a way of blending into the very fabric of a town. Only when it suited him did he appear.

And when he appeared it was usually to kill.

But Trey Skinner did not kill as other men killed.

He never drew down on anyone who could actually defend himself. His was not the skill or raw courage of the legendary gunfighters who braved an opponent in a showdown.

Skinner liked to kill but had no desire to die. When he drew one of his guns it was always against someone who had no chance of bettering him.

He kept well hidden under porch overhangs and store doorways as he continued stealthily to trail the three cowboys. Skinner did not wish to duel with any of them.

He only wanted to kill.

The cowboys eventually reached the stables and walked their horses through its wide-open doors. Skinner gave a cruel twisted smile and nodded to himself. Now that he knew where they were his mind returned to Adams and the three lawmen. He turned and began to retrace his steps through the dimly lit alleys and side-streets until he reached the main thoroughfare once more. His eyes narrowed as he stared at the marshal's office.

He thought about the tall rancher and the veteran marshal for a few moments. They were men who had survived far longer than most and that meant they were dangerous. But neither of the deputies he had seen looked as though they could defend themselves with comparable skill. If he had to choose his next victim it would be one of them, he told himself.

He wiped the drool from his mouth.

Skinner found an unlit alley from where he could gain an uninterrupted view of the building. He leaned against a weathered wall and watched with unblinking eyes.

It was said that once a man had tasted blood he would never lose his craving for it.

The night was still young and the ruthless Skinner was still hungry.

SEVEN

There was a cold wind blowing through the streets of Death, yet little seemed to have altered since the brutal slaying of Clu Brooks. The saloons were still as busy as they had been prior to Skinner's display of his lethal accuracy. Even the Broken Bottle had resumed its normal level of trade within minutes of the cowboy's killing. It was as if nothing had happened at all. When the bucket of sawdust had been thrown over the bloody floor of the popular drinking hole everyone appeared to forget the deadly one-sided shoot-out.

There was a building about 300 yards away from the Broken Bottle which, unlike most of the others which fronted the main thoroughfare, had a fresh coat of paint adorning its brighly decorated façade. This was a place where the better-heeled of the town's residents gathered.

It was a grand place, where money was won and lost and deals were conceived and brought to fruition.

The Diamond Pin gaming hall was one of many along Main Street but, unlike all its competitors, it boasted every member of the Death Cattlemen's Association as founder members. Only the rich entered this establishment. Only they could afford the prices.

Five well-heeled cattlemen gathered most evenings in the well-appointed private room at the rear of the building to play poker and discuss ways in which they might be able to increase their already profitable business ventures. The five ranchers used the fertile range west of town collectively to fatten their herds before sending them north to the Eastern buyers. It had proved to be a most lucrative venture.

Their wealth had originally accumulated from the steers they bred and sold, but it had allowed them to buy stakes in almost all the town's other businesses. It made good sense to the cattlemen that they should own part shares in saloons and brothels, as well as the town's gambling houses, as it allowed them to recoup the wages they paid their cowboys each month.

In a way everyone worked for the five members of the Death Cattlemen's Association. Yet few actually knew it.

Cyril Coltrane was the richest and oldest of the small group. He never permitted anyone to forget that it. Coltrane ruled the roost and made most of the decisions for the small but prosperous fellowship. The others tended to follow his lead, as he had never done anything other than make them richer.

Mort Fuller was the only bachelor in the group. He tended to spend far more time at the card tables than the others. Brad Quinn could have been the richest of them all if it had not been for the sorrowful fact that he had a nagging wife, ten children and three mistresses. Yet for some reason Quinn was almost always seen to be smiling.

Pete Parker liked whiskey, poker and little else. He had never appeared to have a thought of his own when it came to business matters. He just nodded and agreed to anything his partners wanted to do as long as it gave him time to play cards. The seemingly hapless Parker had a wife who liked to spend his money and turned a blind eye to anything her spouse did. Nobody envied him. Unlike Quinn, Parker seldom smiled.

The fifth member of the Cattlemen's Association was called Chuck Foyle. He was a secretive man who had a wife and a twenty-year-old son called Bud. Few ever saw Foyle's boy or, indeed, his wife. There was a rumour that Mrs Foyle was more than ten years older than her rancher husband and that was why she never ventured out during the hours of sunlight. For the rays of a Texas sun did little to enhance the fading looks of a woman desperate to conceal the inevitable ravages of time. Foyle never missed a night at the Diamond Pin, even though he was not a very good card-player; he liked to drink. He really liked to drink.

All five were gathered around the green-baize table with stacks of multicoloured chips before them as the door to the private room burst inward to reveal the stunned face of the town clerk, Horace Matherson.

The five men all lowered their various pipes and cigars from their mouths and stared at the face of the small, weedy Matherson as sweat traced its way from the top of his bald head down to his crooked bow tie. He was shaking as though he had seen the Devil himself.

'H-have you heard?' Matherson gasped.

With obvious signs of outrage, Coltrane stood and adjusted his pot belly beneath his silk vest.

'What are you doing here, Horace?' Coltrane roared. 'This is for members only and you ain't a member! What on earth has gotten you so all-fired up, man?'

Matherson rushed to a table with its array of liquor bottles lined up along its highly polished surface. He swiftly poured himself a glassful and swallowed it in

65

one gulp before returning to the red-faced Coltrane.

'Somebody shot a cowboy over in the Broken Bottle!' Matherson managed to say before sucking in air.

The men all looked at one another in a bemused fashion. It was not as if none of them had ever heard of someone getting shot within the boundaries of Death before.

'So what?' Fuller asked as he tapped the ash from his cigar into a silver tray next to his chips.

'Cowboys get shot all the time.' Quinn shrugged as he counted his own shrinking stack of chips.

'Shot dead!' Matherson added.

'Cowboys are always getting killed.' Coltrane waved a hand at Matherson as though trying to rid the room of an unpleasant stench. 'Go away.'

'This was one of Gene Adams's cowboys,' Matherson blurted out as his left arm pointed behind him at thin air.

Parker stood and wandered with an empty glass to the table where a dozen bottles of whiskey were lined up. He poured himself a good measure, then looked hard at the town clerk.

'Is Adams in town?'

'Damn right he is!' Matherson nodded for emphasis. 'And he ain't happy about one of his hands getting himself shot dead.'

Foyle glanced at the others. 'Adams can be damn

dangerous when his boys get hurt.'

Coltrane walked up to the sweating clerk. 'Who shot this cowboy, Horace?'

'A stranger,' Matherson replied. 'They say his name is Skinner.'

Again the five men looked into each others' faces. If any of them had heard of the name before they managed to hide it well from the others.

'What's Adams doing in Death?' Fuller asked. 'His ranch is fifty miles or more from here.'

Quinn bit his lower lip. 'Whatever his reason for being in Death he sure ain't gonna be happy to lose one of his hands as soon as he arrived.'

'Adams ain't the kind to cross,' Parker said. 'He don't cotton to his boys getting hurt, let alone killed! He'll be mighty sore about this.'

'But he ain't the sort to take the law into his own hands and start trouble, is he?' Foyle wondered.

Fuller stood and walked to the whiskey bottles. 'Ain't he? When Gene Adams came to this land there weren't no law except gun law, Chuck. If he wants to start trouble that's exactly what he'll do.'

'Skinner?' Coltrane repeated the name and rubbed his flabby chin as he wandered thoughtfully around the well-appointed room. He glanced at the others again. 'Skinner! Have any of you hired anyone going by that handle?'

They all shook their heads.

Coltrane moved back to Matherson. 'Where's Adams now?'

'With the marshal.'

'Thank the Lord!' Coltrane blew out his cheeks. 'Harper will calm the old fool down.'

Quinn sipped at his drink. 'The real question is, where's this Skinner varmint? If he'll kill a cowboy none of us is safe!'

Matherson shrugged. 'I don't know where that critter went, gents. He just up and vanished.'

Coltrane looked at the bald man. 'Didn't Harper arrest Skinner?'

'He couldn't,' the clerk said. 'It was self-defence. A dozen people seen Adams's boy draw first.'

'So it was the cowboy's fault?' Foyle sighed.

'That ain't the way I heard it,' Matherson corrected. 'A few folks said that this Skinner dude riled the cowboy up so bad that the young kid lost his head and went for his hogleg. They say that was what this stranger wanted. He just drew and fired one shot and killed the boy dead. But it's still self-defence in the eyes of Texas law. The kid cleared his holster first.'

Coltrane rubbed his throat and placed a silver dollar in the bald man's sweating palm. 'Thank you, Horace. You can go back to your home now. I appreciate the information.'

'Thank you kindly, Mr Coltrane.'

The clerk headed out of the room. Coltrane closed the door behind him and looked at his fellow cattlemen. 'Something ain't right here, boys. I smell a whole heap of trouble in the air. This morning they found old Dan Cooper shot dead up on the mountain and now another cowboy is gunned down. Something's brewing and it ain't coffee.'

'What'll we do?' Parker asked.

'Get your hats,' Coltrane ordered. 'I think we'd better go and see the marshal.'

'And Gene Adams?' Foyle asked.

'And Gene Adams,' Coltrane boomed. 'Come on!'

As always the four other men did exactly as they were instructed. They got their hats then followed the rotund Coltrane as he marched down the corridor.

The hayloft was vast, yet to the three cowboys it felt little better than a prison. The open hatch directly over the stable doors offered an uninterrupted view of the entire town. From this high vantage point a man could see practically every street and alley. Only the shadows where the rays of the waxing moon could not reach managed to keep their mysteries. With moonlight casting its eerie blue hue into the loft Gene Adams's cowboys stared out upon the place where death had struck down their youngest comrade. They still found it difficult to accept that the young cowhand was laid out at the funeral parlour and not still beside them asking his naïve questions.

The thin old-timer, Tomahawk, rested against the edge of the open hatch and held on to a rope which dangled from a pulley just above him. His thumb ran along the honed edge of his Indian hatchet as he wondered whether he might have been able to do something which could have prevented the gunman from striking out at their most vulnerable chum. His wrinkled old eyes had seen a lot of death in his long life, but still it was something that he could not understand.

Johnny Puma walked to the old man's side and sat down. His legs hung and swayed as he too glared out with eyes which could not quite accept what had happened.

'Penny for them?' Johnny asked with a sigh.

'I was thinking that maybe I should have thrown my tomahawk at that varmint back in the saloon, Johnny,' Tomahawk said. 'I could have split his skull open before he—'

'We gonna stay here?' Kelso Scott snarled from behind them as he chewed on a tobacco plug.

'That's the idea,' Johnny answered.

'That's what Gene told us to do, Kelso,' Tomahawk added.

Scott scrambled off the hay and brushed himself

down. He moved to the other men and rested a hand against the weathered wood of the hatchway that framed them.

'I ain't a child! I don't like being treated like one!' Scott fumed as he spat out into the darkness. 'Gene ain't got no right to order us to stay here. Where the hell is he? I reckon he's out there ready to gun that Skinner down himself.'

Tomahawk looked up at the wrangler. 'Don't go getting yourself all worked up. Gene ain't stupid.'

Scott poked Tomahawk's thin bony shoulder. He leaned down. 'You saying I am? You calling me stupid just coz I wanna go out there and make that killer pay?'

Johnny looked up. 'Easy, Kelso. Don't go picking on Tomahawk just coz we have to stay here.'

Scott spat again. 'I don't have to stay here. I'm going to find that bastard and make him draw on me.'

Both Johnny and Tomahawk watched as the burly Scott left them and headed for the ladder.

'What you say?' Tomahawk yelled out.

'You heard me.' Scott grabbed the top of the ladder and placed his right boot on the rung. 'I'm headed back to the Broken Bottle to see if I can get me a trail on the varmint! He's gotta be somewhere in this town!'

Johnny got to his feet fast. He rushed to the ladder

71

just as Scott was starting to make his way down towards where a dozen or more horses were stalled. Johnny grabbed the nearer arm of the wrangler and pulled it hard.

'That's a loco idea!'

'Now you're calling me loco,' Scott snarled, jerking his arm free. 'You might want to sit up here like good little boys but Kelso Scott got himself other ideas!'

Johnny started down the ladder after his raging pal. 'Don't you think me and Tomahawk want to kill that Skinner? But he's fast, Kelso. Damn fast!'

Scott reached the floor and patted his holstered six-shooter as Johnny caught up with him.

'You ain't goin no place!' Johnny reached out and caught Scott's arm. He pulled him back with all his might.

Scott's eyes narrowed. He clenched his right fist, then swung it with all his fury. The punch caught Johnny just under the chin. It was powerful enough to lift the cowboy off his feet and send him flying back into the ladder just as Tomahawk slid to the ground.

The old man hovered above the supine figure of Johnny Puma. He blinked hard, and then looked up. He just caught a glimpse of Scott as the wrangler marched out into the street.

'W-what happened?' Johnny slurred as he nursed

his bruised jaw and vainly tried to get off the dirt floor of the livery.

Tomahawk shook his head and looked down at the cowboy, who had blood pouring from his open mouth.

'Reckon you lost the argument, Johnny boy!'

EIGHT

The lethal gunman Trey Skinner had only just started to notice the change in temperature when he spotted five well-dressed men parading down the main street towards him. Their shadows danced in the coal-tar lantern light that spilled across the churned-up sand as the men crossed the street and aimed their footwear in the direction of Harper's office. Skinner watched, as all creatures with killing in their hearts watch. Riders still rode up and down the street in various stages of drunkenness but they did not see him and he ignored them. His eyes were on the five men as they negotiated the boardwalks toward their goal. For a moment Skinner did nothing, then he stepped closer to the corner of the building opposite the marshal's office. His eyes narrowed as they focused upon the rotund Cyril

Coltrane at the head of the prosperous-looking group.

He stepped out from the alley and up on to the boardwalk of the town's only barber-shop and rested against a wooden upright beneath its porch overhang. The barber had long finished for the day, yet the smell of pomade and shaving-soap still hung in the night air. There were no lights on inside the empty store, which allowed the curious gunman to watch the approaching line of men from the shadows without them seeing him.

Skinner smiled. It was the sickly smile he always wore when preparing to kill. His right hand stroked the wooden grip of his gun for a few seconds, then his index finger slid into the weapon's guard and hooked into its trigger. Skinner pulled the gun free of its holster and raised it up to his face. The cold steel felt good against his cheekbone.

'This'll be like stealing candy from a baby,' he muttered to himself as his thumb carefully pulled back the Colt's hammer until it fully locked into position. The clicks of the weapon's mechanism beside his ear made his smile grow wider. 'All I gotta figure is which one I'll plug first.'

It was a choice he relished making. The ruthless man who used the rule of law to enable him to slaughter and mock those who witnessed his deadly accuracy nodded as he made up his mind.

He had chosen.

Skinner straightened his arm.

He aimed.

He fired.

A plume of gunsmoke encircled the barrel.

A white-hot flash of lead spat out and tore through the air as it sought out its target. The resounding shot echoed all along the wide street. The five men stopped in their tracks just as they reached the marshal's office. They all looked to where only a cloud of gunsmoke lingered on the night air: the only evidence that Skinner had been there at all.

The door to the office opened and Marshal Harper, Adams and the two deputies rushed out into the street, Coltrane looked around at his colleagues and was about to speak when he saw the grim expression etched on the face of Chuck Foyle. A trail of blood ran down from the corner of the man's mouth. He was spluttering, his eyes wide open.

'Foyle!' Coltrane gasped.

But Foyle did not hear the call of his name. He had been directly behind the burly Coltrane, but even Coltrane's vast expanse of flesh had not been enough to save him. He staggered and fell into the arms of Mort Fuller, then slid to the boards.

'He's dead!' Fuller exclaimed.

Marshal Harper looked at his deputies, then shouted his orders at them. He pointed his gun to where the gunsmoke still hung. 'Get after him! He must have run up that alley.'

Jones and Tork held their rifles close to their chests and dashed across the street. Jones pointed at fresh boot-prints and both men rushed up into the dark alley. They would seek him out, but men like Skinner were not so easily captured.

Gene Adams had not drawn his weapons. They remained in their holsters as the seasoned rancher walked to where the dead man lay. He knelt and then pulled Foyle's tailed coat open. His eyes stared at the single bullet hole in the white shirt as blood quickly turned the fine cotton a dark crimson.

With a knowing glance Adams looked at the four other members of the association. Adams knew all of them well. He looked hard into their stunned faces and raised an eyebrow.

'Chuck's a gonner! Any of you see who did this?' he asked. He straightened up to his full height.

They all shook their heads.

'What about you, Coltrane?' Adams pressed. 'You were at the head of this bunch. Didn't you see the shooter?'

'Nope! I didn't see anyone, Adams,' Coltrane managed to answer. 'It all happened so damn fast. We weren't expecting no one to be lying in wait for us.'

Adams looked down at the body. 'Reckon you

figured that only cowboys ended up that way.'

Parker was shaking. He turned and supported himself against a wooden upright as he choked on his own vomit for a few moments.

'Who would have done this, Gene?' Quinn edged closer to the tall rancher who was staring out from beneath the brim of his black ten-gallon hat and studying the street carefully.

Adams's eyes darted to Quinn. 'Looks like the work of a maniac to me, Brad. But I'd not bet on it.'

'What you mean, Adams?' Fuller asked.

'Looks can be deceptive,' Adams replied. 'Innocent folks getting themselves killed for no reason seems like the work of a locobean, but I ain't so sure.'

Marshal Harper stepped back up on to the boardwalk and rubbed his neck as he looked down upon the dead Foyle. The blood had spread out across the once pristine shirt-front. It glistened in the flickering lantern light that cascaded out from the open door of the marshal's office.

'Heart-shot again, Gene,' Harper noted wryly.

'Yep!' Adams nodded in agreement. 'Just the way Skinner killed my boy.'

'And exactly the way Cooper was gunned down up on the mountainside,' Harper added.

Cyril Coltrane followed his massive belly to the two men and pointed a finger at them both in turn. 'If you know who did this, arrest him. That's what we pay you for, Don. Go and do your duty and arrest the culprit.'

'And we'll have him hanging from a tree before sunup,' Fuller grunted.

Harper looked at the fat man, then at the three others behind him. Parker had vomit hanging on his chin as he steadied himself behind the others.

'And how exactly do I prove Skinner did this, Cyril?'

'Catch him!' Parker demanded. 'Then we'll string him up.'

'That's why I got my deputies chasing shadows,' Harper said in a low tone designed to trouble those who attempted to tell him his job. 'But unless we catch the man with the smoking gun I can't prove anything against this Skinner varmint. He shot one of Gene's boys but the law says it was self-defence. Poor old Coop and Foyle here might have themselves the same single bullet hole in their chests but that ain't proof. We might have ourselves another mighty fine shot in Death. We could string Skinner up and still have us a killer on the loose.'

'But you said that the wounds were exactly the same,' Quinn offered.

Adams turned away. 'The marshal's right. That don't mean the same man killed all three.'

Coltrane looked around the street. Now every

79

shadow made him nervous. He edged closer to Adams.

'Kill this Skinner, Adams,' Coltrane said. 'Kill him and we'll pay you a fortune.'

Gene Adams glanced at the fat man. 'I already got me a fortune, Coltrane. Besides, I don't kill for money.'

Suddenly Kelso Scott came running from around the corner. The wrangler slowed, then spotted the men standing in the light from the office and street-lanterns. He raced along the street to the tallest among the group.

'What happened, Gene?' he gasped. 'I heard shooting!'

'What are you doing here, Kelso?' Adams growled. 'I told you and the others to stay in the livery 'til I got there.'

Scott spotted the body lying in a pool of blood. His eyes returned to his boss. 'Another one?'

'Yep! Another one, Kelso,' Adams replied. 'This time our killer went for a rich'un instead of a cowpoke.'

Scott's teeth gritted. 'I'm gonna go kill that Skinner. His killing days are over.'

Adams grabbed hold of his wrangler's muscular arm and pulled him close. He stared into Scott's angry eyes.

'You ain't killing no one, boy! Hear me?'

80

Scott broke free and patted his holstered Colt. 'I sure am, Gene. He ain't gonna kill nobody else.'

'That's the spirit, young man.' Coltrane, smiling, pushed himself closer to the pair of arguing men. 'We shall pay you a hundred dollars if you—'

'Just a damn minute here, Cyril,' Marshal Harper interrupted. 'You can't go waving your wallet around like that!'

Scott looked at the four men. 'A hundred bucks?'

'I'm ordering you to get back to the livery, Kelso,' Adams shouted. 'You ain't killing anyone for money.'

'Who said? You might be scared, Gene. But I ain't,' Scott said loudly. 'If these slickers wanna pay me for doing something I was gonna do anyways, what's the difference?'

'The difference is that you ain't no gunfighter, boy,' Adams raged. 'You'll get killed for sure.'

'Two hundred!' Coltrane revised.

Gene Adams pushed Scott aside and grabbed hold of Coltrane's coat collar. He clenched his gloved hand and punched the cattleman on one of his numerous chins. Coltrane tumbled backwards, fell off the boardwalk and landed on his rear next to the trough. The well-rounded man rubbed his aching face and then aimed a finger at Scott.

'A thousand dollars, boy! Kill this maniac and we'll pay you a thousand in cash!'

'You got yourself a deal,' Scott told him.

81

Don Harper turned to Adams. 'Can't you control your damn cowboys, Gene?'

'Can't you control your rich folks?' Adams snapped back.

The three cattlemen helped Coltrane back to his feet. They glared at the man with the star pinned to his chest and then at the tall rancher.

'If you can't handle this, Harper, we can!' Coltrane sneered.

Adams was about to speak when the wrangler turned his back on him and started to walk away. 'I quit, Gene! I ain't gonna work for anyone who don't right a wrong when he has to. Young Clu is gonna be avenged!'

Tomahawk and Johnny came around the corner and looked at Scott as he marched away in the direction of the nearest saloon.

The four cattlemen turned and also began to file away. Gene Adams rubbed his knuckles across his mouth.

Harper shook his head. 'That cowboy any good with his gun, Gene?'

'You know many cowpunchers who can use their guns, Don?'

'Nope!'

'There's your answer, old friend.' Adams stepped over the body and moved towards Tomahawk and Johnny. Neither of the cowboys had ever seen their

82

boss looking quite so frustrated before.

'What's going on, Gene boy?' Tomahawk asked.

Adams did not answer.

NINE

Clutching their Winchesters firmly in their hands the deputies had moved around the back lanes of half a dozen buildings following the trail of boot-prints in the sand left by the fleeing Skinner. The marks were clear and easily made out by the pair of lawmen but the older of the two had started to feel uneasy. The thought occurred to him that they might not be hunting the unseen gunman at all. The tracks might in fact be bait which had lured them into the darkest recesses of the town called Death.

Were they they the hunters or the prey?

Silently, Ben Jones raised a hand and stopped his younger companion at the very edge of the well-secured yard belonging to the Red Branch saloon. Clevis Tork was about to speak when the moonlight caught the older deputy's face. He contained his questions and watched the more experienced man as

Jones pointed the long barrel of his rifle at the ground.

Tork moved closer.

Then he too saw what Jones had spotted.

The boot-prints led straight to the saloon's high rear gate, then stopped. They were the marks of boots which had walked and not run to this spot. The gate and its fence stood at least seven feet tall and had a line of barbed wire running across its top. Jones dropped on to one knee and squinted hard at the impressions. Tork copied the action.

'This don't make no sense, Clevis boy,' Jones whispered. 'No damn sense at all!'

'What don't?'

Again Jones pointed at the marks left in the sand. The deep marks of Skinner's boots led right up to the gate but showed no sign that the man had cut up the sand to climb the gate. Both deputies stood up and Jones used his left hand to lift the hefty chain and padlock. It was firmly secured.

He stared at it.

'I don't cotton to this at all!'

'Maybe the gate was open when the killer got here, Ben,' Tork suggested. 'Maybe he closed the gate and then locked it after him?'

Jones raised an eyebrow and tilted his head. He looked straight at the younger man and waved the padlock in his hand.

'You reckon? Then how come this was locked up from the outside, Clevis? If the gate had bin open and the man locked it with this old padlock it'd be on the inside of the yard. Right?'

'What?' Tork leaned closer to the padlock in his partner's hand. A pained expression came over his face. His eyes met those of Jones. 'Damn it all, you're right! Whoever locked this gate up would have to have bin on the outside, right where we're standing. I don't get it.'

Jones released the lock and chain. It banged against the sturdy wooden gate as he turned and looked around the alley, as if hoping that answers to his many unvoiced questions might appear. There were no miraculous answers. Two sturdy broad-leafed trees flanked the alley to their right. A place where they had not yet ventured. Even the bright moon failed to illuminate the ground beyond that point.

'Where in tarnation did he go?' Jones snarled as his finger teased the trigger of his rifle. 'Men don't just vanish into thin air like this. He came this way but. . . .'

The young Tork looked up. The cruel wire which topped the fence and gate glistened in the eerie blue light of the moon above them.

'Could he have jumped up there and gotten over that wire without cutting himself to shreds, Ben?' he wondered.

'If he was a bird.' Jones continued to study the maze of fenced alleyways which surrounded them, then looked at his fellow law officer. 'I ain't too sure of anything any more, Clevis. I'd bet a week's salary that no man could jump up and over that gate without leaving the marks in the sand or cutting himself up something awful. But now I ain't sure he didn't do just that.'

'It's impossible,' Tork muttered.

'For a normal person it's impossible, but what if this killer ain't normal?' Jones felt a cold shiver tracing his spine. 'What if this killer is something we ain't tackled before?'

'Like a ghost?' Tork lowered his chin until it touched the knot of his bandanna. 'You trying to tell me we're chasing a ghost, Ben?'

'Some crazy folks are as strong as bulls, Clevis,' Jones told him. 'What if this 'un can leap around like some of them *hombres* who work in the circus or freak shows?'

'You figure?' Tork gulped and glanced around them. Sweat defied the cold breeze which swept along the alley and trailed down his young face. 'Let's get back to the marshal, Ben! I've had my fill of this damn alley.'

'You and me both,' Jones agreed. 'I'd hate for him to pick us off the way he shot old Foyle!'

They both turned to retrace their steps when

suddenly a sound came from the shadows beyond the trees. Deep in the narrow fenced alley where even the moonlight could not penetrate, something was moving.

'What the hell was that?' Tork gasped as he swung around and aimed his rifle barrel into the blackness. 'You hear it?'

'I heard it, Clevis.' Jones screwed up his eyes and cranked the mechanism of his repeating rifle into action. It was cocked and ready. 'C'mon, Clevis! Let's go find out what that is.'

'B-but what if it is a ghost or some kinda freak like you said.' Tork reluctantly kept step with his fellow deputy. 'I ain't sure we got the right kind of bullets to bring down no ghost, Ben.'

'Me neither, but maybe we'll find out what we've bin trailing for the last ten minutes.' Jones gritted his teeth and continued into the blackness. 'C'mon, boy!'

Both men walked away from the gate and headed into the alley of dark shadows. The strange noise grew louder.

It beckoned them.

They obeyed its luring call.

The silence was deafening. With Tomahawk and Johnny to either side of him Gene Adams had barely uttered a word since the three men had entered the

88

still busy Red Branch saloon. Propped up against the long wet bar counter the tall rancher simply stared into the mirror behind the bartender at his own blurred reflection. Tomahawk aimed a bony finger at the man with the apron wrapped around his waist and indicated for their glasses to be refilled. Always a man to oblige good customers, Joe White brought the whiskey bottle to the bearded old-timer and expertly filled the trio of small glasses.

'Leave the bottle, Joe,' Adams said tossing a few coins at the bartender.

'Sure enough,' White nodded, placed the bottle of rye down between them and scooped up the money. Noisy customers at the other end of the saloon drew him away before he could say anything else.

'Y'know something?' Johnny said. 'I think I like beer better than this paint thinner!'

'You're getting soft, you young whippersnapper!' Tomahawk said with a toothless smile on his face.

'Just drink!' Adams sighed.

In a vain attempt to be as tall as Adams Tomahawk stood on the brass bar rail, wrinkled up his eyes and stared long and hard at the troubled rancher beside him.

'Now don't go thinking that I'm a mite ungrateful, Gene boy,' Tomahawk started. 'But I've known you for forty years or more and I ain't never seen you drink whiskey before, let alone share any with us cowhands.'

Adams swallowed his drink and refilled his glass. 'You grumbling, old-timer? You've bin nagging me for them same forty years to let you drink whiskey. So drink it!'

'Nope, I ain't grumbling. But I am a little worried.' Tomahawk admitted.

Adams pushed the bottle to his oldest friend then turned to face the other patrons in the saloon. He watched the bar girls as they plied their trade around the tables, then he looked at the various groups of menfolk. Some were happy and it showed. Some were troubled and that also showed. Some men were neither but ready to see what the next hand of cards might bring to them. Thoughtfully Adams lowered his head.

'You ever bin in a situation like this before, boys?'

With a sour expression on his face, Johnny sipped at his whiskey, then set the glass down. He looked up at the side of the rancher's face. Even with the wide hat brim pulled almost down to the eyebrows it was clear that, for the first time in his entire life, Gene Adams was totally perplexed.

'I ain't never thought that this kinda thing could happen, Gene. A brilliant gunman kills for no reason and yet manages to use the law to keep him from having his neck stretched.'

'What about Chuck Foyle?' Adams asked. 'If this was the handiwork of that Skinner varmint, then why did he shoot him as well?'

'And the cowboy outside town,' Tomahawk added. 'Why'd he get himself killed?'

Johnny rubbed his mouth. 'Maybe Skinner was just practising with that Cooper critter. Getting himself all-fired up so that his trigger finger didn't let him down.'

'It still don't make no sense at all.' Tomahawk downed his drink and ran a tongue around his whiskers like a cat that has just finished the cream.

'It has to be Skinner that killed all three of these men,' Adams whispered just loud enough for his companions to hear. 'But why?'

Johnny rested his hands on his own pair of guns. 'Could be that Skinner is loco like them folks said. Maybe he don't need to have a reason to kill. He just up and kills!'

Adams heaved a long sigh. 'Reckon so. No sane man can ever work out what's going on in a maniac's head! Maybe he *is* killing just because he can.'

Tomahawk tossed another glass of rye into his mouth. 'Only another fool would try and figure out a locobean.'

'We ought to be trying to find Kelso, Gene.' Johnny looked up at the tobacco-stained wall clock. It was almost eight.

Adams made a swift intake of breath. 'Why? He up and quit. He ain't one of us any longer, boys.'

'You don't mean that.' Tomahawk filled his glass again. 'He's mixed up, Gene boy. That Coltrane galoot waved a mighty big carrot under his nose and no mistake.'

'And Kelso was real upset by Clu getting shot.' Johnny added as he changed feet on the brass rail. 'He was teaching Clu all the tricks of his trade and the kid was learning. When Skinner shot him it hurt Kelso bad.'

Tomahawk patted the rancher's arm. 'Johnny's right, Gene. Kelso was with a girl upstairs in the Broken Bottle when the ruckus broke out. I figure he reckons that if'n he'd stayed with us that Skinner wouldn't have picked on Clu.'

'Guilt,' Adams drawled. 'We all know how that can chew up a man's craw.'

Johnny stepped away from the bar. 'Let's go see if we can find Kelso. Maybe stop him from trying his luck.'

Adams nodded. He placed his glass down and started through the crowded saloon towards the swing doors, with Johnny at his left shoulder. 'You're right, boys. C'mon!'

Tomahawk downed his drink, plucked up the whiskey bottle and was about to follow them when he heard Adams's powerful voice bellow out above the din of the crowd.

'Leave that bottle there, Tomahawk. You've had enough.'

The bearded older man's face seemed to scrunch up when he heard Adams's order. He banged the bottle down and sniffed at the laughing bartender.

'Me and my big toothless mouth!' Tomahawk scurried in pursuit through the crowd. 'Reckon it'll be another forty years before I gets to drink my fill of whiskey again!'

As the three men stepped out on to the boardwalk the deafening sound of shots rang out in the evening air. Just as Adams turned he saw the marshal emerge from his office down the long street.

'Where'd them shots come from, Gene?' Harper called out.

Before the rancher could reply, another brace of shots filled the air and echoed all around them.

'That came from behind the saloon, Gene,' Johnny said confidently.

'The boy's right, Gene boy,' Tomahawk agreed.

'You're right!' Gene Adams pulled one of his Colts from its holster and clawed its hammer back. He headed to the side of the building. 'C'mon!'

TEN

The blistering gunfire still echoed all around Death as Gene Adams led his two men along the side of the saloon into the lanes where the only illumination was moonlight. They did not slow their pace until they reached the saloon's yard. Like an ominous warning of how lethal shadows could be to the unwary, the acrid stench of gunsmoke hung on the night air. The tall rancher halted and rested his broad back against the high wooden fencing as the more agile Johnny ran to the opposite side of the narrow enclosure. It was like a labyrinth to the men who had never strayed from the main streets of the town before. Tomahawk had already pulled his Indian hatchet free from his belt. He clutched its leather-bound handle as he sidled up to Adams.

'Where'd you figure the shooting come from, Gene boy?' the old-timer asked as they heard the heavy boots of the marshal running up behind them. Like a dog too old for the chase Harper was panting when he stopped next to Adams.

The shooting seemed to have stopped but there was no guarantee that it might not start up again at any moment. Adams looked at the alleys that went off in three different directions. Then his eyes narrowed and stared into the blackness beyond the large trees. For some reason he instinctively knew that that had to be the place from where the shooting came.

'Have you seen or heard anything?' the marshal asked as he held his long-barrelled .45 in his hand.

Again Adams did not reply. He saw no point in answering questions until he had figured a situation out. Then suddenly half a dozen brilliant flashes lit up the blackness of the lane to their right as deafening gunfire erupted once more. Two bullet tapers cut across the cold air before them at chest height. The fencing stopped the lead, which sent wood shavings exploding into the air. Adams narrowed his eyes.

'There's your answer, Don,' Adams said before moving across the sand to the nearest of the big trees. Before he had time to fill his lungs the three other men were at his side. More shots rang out. 'Ain't no way we can head on up there without getting ourselves plugged!'

'I heard me rifle fire as well as a six-shooter, Gene,'

Johnny said firmly.

'Your deputies got Winchesters, Don? Right?' Adams drawled.

'Yep,' Harper confirmed it.

'That means that our marksman ain't managed to kill with a single shot this time,' Adams mused. 'This time he's failed to execute his victims and has found himself in a battle!'

'My boys are still alive?' the marshal said hopefully.

'One of them is anyways,' Adams answered. 'But I figure if any of us try to get to them we'll be picked off before we get within ten yards of them!'

'You're right, Gene boy,' Tomahawk agreed. 'With the moon on our backs we'd be eating lead as soon as we got in there!'

Johnny had an idea. He turned to the lawman. 'Is there another way to get to the end of this lane, Marshal?'

Harper nodded firmly. 'Sure is, Johnny. C'mon and follow me and we'll circle around. We might be able to get the drop on whoever it is doing all the shooting.'

'Good idea,' Adams said.

Both Johnny and Harper swung round on their heels and ran towards Main Street.

Tomahawk leaned closer to the rancher. 'Them young deputies must have gotten themselves bushwhacked! What kinda yella-belly we after, Gene?'

96

'A real bad'un, old-timer,' Adams replied with a sigh.

The old man looked troubled. 'How we gonna help them boys? We's stuck here. Ain't no way we can git in there. Even if we tries to shoot into that lane we might hit them young lawmen.'

Adams took a deep breath and stepped right up to the big tree. He removed his hat and tossed it away before leaning round the tree's trunk. Even his keen eyesight could not make out anything in the fence-lined lane. The rancher raised his left hand and cupped it to the side of his mouth.

'Ben! Clevis!' Adams called out loudly. 'You boys OK?'

For a moment there was no reply. Then he heard the muffled moan of a man who was obviously worse for wear. Whatever the deputy was trying to say his words were muffled in agony.

'That boy's hurt, Gene!' Tomahawk said. 'Hurt bad by the sound of it.'

Adams gritted his teeth nodded. 'At least he ain't dead!'

Tomahawk touched Adams's sleeve. 'I thought there was two deputies on the tail of that killer, Gene boy. I only heard one man groan.'

Again Adams nodded. 'Yeah! I got me a bad feeling about that, Tomahawk.'

'You figure one of them young 'uns is dead?'

97

'If we wait any longer they'll both be buzzard bait, Tomahawk.'

'What you thinking of doing, boy?' Tomahawk had recognized the tone in his pal's voice. He had heard it many times over the previous few decades and it usually came just before the tall man did something dangerous. 'Answer me, Gene. What you got festering in that head of yours?'

Gene Adams checked both his guns carefully. They were both fully loaded and ready for action. He looked down at the old-timer beside him and smiled.

'There's only one way to find out if them boys are dead or alive, old-timer!' Adams defied his own logical mind, pushed one of his six-shooters into the bony hand of his pal, turned and began to run into the blackness to where they had heard the wounded deputy moaning. 'Cover me!'

Tomahawk blinked hard and then gulped.

Although an expert with his Indian hatchet he was notorious for his inability even to hit the sky with a bullet. But Tomahawk did as he had been instructed and started to fire the Colt carefully over the head of the rancher. With every flash of lead venom that spewed from the barrel of the gun in his hand Tomahawk caught a brief glimpse of Adams as the tall man continued his run towards his unseen goal.

Shots were returned from the depths of the long alley. Each bullet was aimed at Adams as he defiantly ran onwards. Tomahawk saw the rancher throw himself on to the ground and begin to return fire. Once more the confines of the fenced alley lit up with fiery battle.

'Good boy!' the old man muttered gleefully. 'You git that dirty sidewinder and make him pay!'

ELEVEN

The sound of the gunfire ended as quickly as it had erupted yet the echoes rang out for what seemed like an eternity along the narrow wood-fenced alleyways. After running 300 yards along Main Street, Harper led Johnny down the narrow gap between the Silver Dollar gambling house and a hardware store. When both men reached the back of the two buildings they emerged into an alley, the very one that led to the place where the deputies had walked into an ambusher's bullets less than ten minutes earlier. Gunsmoke wafted up into the night air as the men entered the start of the fenced up area.

The marshal had his gun cocked and ready. Johnny simply rested his hands on the two grips of the guns in his holsters. They entered the darkest part of the alley like men approaching their own gallows. Neither spoke. They simply listened and narrowed their eyes in a vain attempt to see the gunman they sought.

They had gone fifty yards when Harper abruptly halted. For the first time since leaving Gene Adams the lawman opened his mouth and swiftly glanced at his younger companion.

'Listen up!' he whispered. 'You hear that?'

Johnny Puma stopped in his tracks and did what the older man advised. He tilted his head and listened.

Then he nodded.

'I hear it.'

The sound that both men had heard appeared to be getting louder with every passing beat of their racing hearts. Johnny drew one of his guns and cocked its hammer as quietly as he could. The gun hung beside his right leg as the cowboy took another step.

Both men were at the corner of a high wooden wall. Unlike the opposite end of the alley, where the fencing looked newly erected, this portion of fencing was weathered and rotten. The planks of lumber were riddled with holes big enough for a grown man to escape through in at least half a dozen places to both sides of them.

'Somebody's coming, Marshal. I hear boots,' Johnny said in a low tone.

Harper nodded in acknowledgement and watched as the cowboy raised his arm until the .45 was level with his hip. 'Let him come! He'll be eating lead before he gets the drop on us.'

'Easy, Johnny!' the marshal urged. 'We gotta make sure we don't go killing the wrong person!'

Johnny inhaled deeply. 'I sure wish there was a tad more light along here, Marshal. I can't see hardly nothing at all but I sure can hear him.'

Harper brushed next to the leaner man. 'Let me handle this.'

'If you get plugged I'll kill the varmint fast!'

The footsteps grew louder and louder. They sounded as though they belonged to a man who was dragging his feet for some reason. It sounded as if a drunk was approaching them. If not a drunk then possibly a man who was wounded.

'Whoever that is he's sure taking his own sweet time about it,' Johnny complained. His finger curled in readiness around the trigger of his cocked .45.

'Easy, Johnny,' Harper said. He moved out from the cover of the corner of the fence behind which they had both been standing.

Although the experienced lawman still could not see who was approaching them he knew that whoever it was must now be close.

'This is Marshal Harper,' the marshal said loudly. 'Raise them hands and git here! One false move and make no mistake about it, we'll blow you to bits!'

The laboured steps kept on coming.

'You hear me?' Harper yelled.

'I hear you, Don! I ain't deaf!'

Suddenly out of the shadows Gene Adams emerged with the body of one of the deputies in his arms. Blood dripped like rain from the unconscious man he cradled.

Harper gasped and holstered his gun. He ran to the rancher and took hold of the deputy in his own powerful arms. Even the darkness could not hide the features of Ben Jones from his wrinkled eyes.

'Is he dead, Gene?'

'Nearly,' Adams replied. 'He needs a doctor damn bad!'

'What about Clevis?' Harper forced himself to ask even though he did not really want to know the obvious answer. 'Is he dead?'

Adams lowered his head. 'Yep! Real dead!'

'I gotta get this boy to the doc's.' The marshal began to head back towards Main Street with the wounded deputy in his strong arms. 'I gotta get him there fast!'

Johnny moved beyond Adams. His gun was still aimed down into the blackness of the lane. He swung back and grabbed hold of the rancher's left arm. Adams looked at the cowboy.

'Did you get the bastard that done this, Gene?' Johnny asked. 'Is his carcass lying back there with Clevis?'

103

'Nope,' Adams sighed regretfully. 'Whoever it was just vanished into thin air.'

Johnny looked at the breaks in the wooden fence which flanked them on both sides. 'A buffalo could have high-tailed it through some of them holes, Gene.'

'Yep!'

'What we gonna do?'

'First we'll go back and pick up what's left of young Clevis and take him to the funeral parlour.' Adams began to retrace his steps with the cowboy at his side. 'We'll get Tomahawk on the way.'

'Then what we gonna do?' the cowboy asked.

Adams rubbed his face with a gloved hand. 'I reckon we ought to find that Skinner critter and check them guns of his, Johnny. If it was him that did this his Colts ought to be mighty damn hot!'

'And if they are, I'll kill him, Gene,' Johnny said.

The rancher glanced at the young cowboy. 'The thing is, I got me a gnawing in my craw about this, Johnny. We seen how accurate that Skinner is with his hogleg. I can't see how he'd get himself mixed up in a real dangerous battle like that was. He could have just picked them boys off someplace else. One shot per deputy!'

'Yeah!' Johnny dropped his gun into its holster when they reached the blood-covered ground. The moon had moved higher in the black sky above

104

them. Now its bluish light was bathing the lane in all its glory. But the sight which greeted both men was not glorious.

It was hideous.

Even the hardened Adams felt sick at what his eyes saw lying at their feet. He rubbed his face with his hands and inhaled deeply.

What remained of Clevis Tork was almost unrecognizable.

'Look at him, Johnny,' Adams mumbled. 'He's riddled with bullets from head to toe!'

'This sure don't match up to all them other dead 'uns we've bin tripping over, Gene,' Johnny observed.

'It sure don't, boy!'

Silently they leaned down and picked the limp body off the blood-soaked sand and began to carry it back to where they knew Tomahawk waited. With Adams at the shoulders of the deputy and Johnny at the legs the men carefully made their way along the alley towards Tomahawk's thin figure.

'I don't get this. Do you think that there's another gunman in town killing folks besides Skinner, Gene?' Johnny asked as they reached the bearded old-timer. 'Is that possible?'

Adams did not reply. His face was like stone.

'What's wrong, Gene?' Johnny pressed.

'I was thinking about Kelso, boy,' Adams answered

with a sigh. 'We still ain't found that hothead.'

'And if we don't and Kelso finds Skinner first, he's a dead man!' Johnny added. 'There ain't no way that wrangler can take on someone like Skinner.'

Tomahawk picked Adams's hat off the ground and moved towards the two men as they laboured on towards the main street.

'Kelso was just here,' he announced.

Adams's eyes narrowed. 'He was?'

'Yep, he sure was!' Tomahawk pointed in the direction they were headed. 'The whippersnapper was looking for that Skinner varmint and he said he'd try his luck at the hotel. He sure wants to earn that thousand dollars!'

Adams and Johnny quickened their pace.

'There's only one kinda luck that boy is gonna find if he does catch up with that gunman and it's all bad!' the rancher exclaimed and spat vigorously on the ground.

TWELVE

They had delivered their pitiful cargo into the hands of the overworked undertaker. Yet their job was still not done. Now they had to attempt to find Scott and prevent him from making the same mistake that Clu Brooks had made. Johnny closed the undertaker's door behind them and stood on the boardwalk beside Tomahawk and the brooding Adams. The young cowboy edged towards the rancher as Adams stepped down on to the sand and made towards the distant hotel. There was purpose in the gait of the tall rancher as he led his men.

His long strides ate up the ground through the amber shafts of lanternlight that spilled across the street.

'Ease up, Gene boy,' Tomahawk pleaded, panting. 'I ain't got the wind I used to have.'

'Ain't no time for us to dawdle, old-timer,' Adams

said over his shoulder. 'For all we know that dumb cowpuncher is already squaring up to Skinner. We have to stop the crazy fool before he ends up back there like the others.'

The street was still busy. A stagecoach thundered past them on its way to the Wells Fargo depot but the three men did not even notice its passage.

'C'mon!' Adams growled.

'Gene!' Johnny quickened and then grabbed hold of Adams by the left arm and stopped him. 'Hold on up!'

Adams turned and looked furiously into Johnny's eyes. 'What the blazes did you do that for?'

Johnny raised an eyebrow and pointed a finger towards the porch outside the marshal's office. The rancher snorted like one of his prize bulls and then focused on the man who sat on a hardback chair outside Harper's office.

'Ain't that Skinner?' Johnny asked.

Adams jaw dropped. 'It sure looks like him.'

'That's the cold-blooded bastard OK!' Tomahawk pulled his hatchet from his belt and moved to the rancher's side. 'Let me split his skull open with my axe, Gene boy!'

'Put that toothpick away.' The rancher pulled Tomahawk back, then he walked across the moonlit sand towards the figure sitting beneath the porch overhang. With Johnny and Tomahawk on either

108

side of him Adams marched up the edge of the water trough and then rested a hand on the hitching rail.

Skinner was sitting with the chair up close against the wall of the building. His eyes glinted in the reflected light that danced off the full trough.

'You looking for me?' Skinner asked quietly.

Adams nodded firmly.

'Yep! I'm looking for you, Skinner.'

'Why?' Skinner leaned forward and rested his hands on his knees. Then he rose to his feet. 'I ain't got no business with any of you critters.'

'Let me kill him, Gene!' Johnny snarled.

Adams raised an arm and pushed the young cowboy back. 'Easy, Johnny! This ain't the sort of man you want to get riled up against you.'

Skinner smiled. It was the same sickly smile that he had displayed moments before gunning down Clu Brooks earlier that evening. He stepped to the edge of the boardwalk and rested his left shoulder against the wooden upright as he flexed the fingers of his right hand above the holstered wooden gun grip.

'You got brains, old man!' Skinner said to Adams.

Adams nodded. 'Two deputies were gunned down in an alley over yonder, Skinner. You happen to know anything about that?'

Skinner shrugged.

'Nope.'

Tomahawk pushed forward and pointed a bony

finger at the smiling man.

'I reckon you're lying!'

Again Gene Adams was forced to push one of his men backwards, away from the man who he knew could administer lethal punishment faster than most could blink an eye.

'If you are innocent of shooting those boys then prove it, Skinner,' Adams drawled.

Skinner raised an eyebrow and looked curiously at the rancher in front of him. 'How does a man prove he didn't do something?'

Adams reached out across the trough with his left hand. 'Give me your guns!'

The smile grew wider on Skinner's twisted face. 'And then you'll shoot me! I ain't stupid, old man. My guns stay with me and that's the way it is. Any of you make a play and I'll oblige you with my own brand of self-defence.'

'I want to check them Colts of yours,' Adams insisted. 'A lot of lead was fired by the *hombre* who shot those deputies. Guns get hot and real dirty during that amount of gunplay.'

Tomahawk leaned close to Adams. 'He could have cleaned them!'

'There ain't bin the time,' Adams argued. 'The shooting only ended a few minutes back.'

'Gene's right,' Johnny agreed, nodding. 'There ain't bin enough time for him to clean his guns if'n he did it.'

Skinner straightened up. 'So if I hand my guns over and you see they ain't bin cleaned up you'll know that I ain't the varmint who shot them lawmen. Right?'

'Yep.'

'I still don't trust any of you three.'

Adams felt the same. 'One gun at a time will do fine.'

All three men watched as Skinner lifted the Colt from his left holster and tossed it into the rancher's hands. His expression never altered. The smile remained carved across his features like a scar.

'Satisfied?' Skinner asked.

Adams could not detect any sign that this weapon had been used in weeks. He threw the gun back and watched the gunman drop it back into the hand-tooled holster.

'The other one,' Adams said.

Skinner pulled the .45 from its leather holster and cast it over the trough into the waiting hands.

'You recall that I used that 'un a while back?'

Adams gritted his teeth angrily. 'I recall!'

Tomahawk and Johnny watched as Adams opened the cylinder and looked at the fresh bullets in its six chambers.

'I reloaded that one!' Skinner said.

Adams nodded. 'I can tell.'

'Well?' Johnny asked.

Adams snapped the cylinder back into the body of the gun and glanced at both of his cowboys in turn. There was a look of frustration on his face. Frustration tinted with confusion.

'Neither of his guns has been used the way the bushwhacker used his guns on Ben and Clevis, boys,' Adams said. 'Whoever gunned them boys down it sure weren't Skinner!'

'What?' Johnny gasped.

'They're pretty clean. One has a hint of being used but that's because our friend here gunned down Clu!'

Skinner caught his weapon and holstered it. 'Satisfied?'

'I won't be satisfied until you're dead, Skinner!' Adams turned away and led his men towards the hotel at the end of the street.

Johnny looked back. To his surprise Skinner had now disappeared into the shadows.

'The varmint's gone!'

'Rats tend to scurry around a lot!' Tomahawk remarked with a sniff.

'It had to be him!' Johnny raged. 'Maybe he got himself another set of guns hidden someplace?'

Adams looked hard at the cowboy. 'Now you're clutching at straws, Johnny. If there is another killer in this town we'd better try and find him before he sends somebody else to boot hill.'

Tomahawk grabbed on to the rancher's coat tail. 'Slow up, Gene boy. I'm tuckered.'

'C'mon! We still gotta find Kelso,' Adams urged.

They had barely taken another six strides when ahead of them six shots rang out and echoed all around them.

'Damn!' Adams snarled.

'Here we go again!' Johnny said.

THIRTEEN

The sight which greeted the three cowboys outside the hotel was totally unexpected. Lying on his back in the street, bathed in the light of the building's porch lanterns Kelso Scott still gripped his smoking gun as he twisted and turned on the ground. The fact that the wrangler was still alive was something none of the three would even have considered possible if he had gone up against the gunman they had left down the street only moments earlier.

This was not the handiwork of the deadly accurate Skinner but the work of someone of lesser skill.

Adams knelt down and gripped the shoulders of the snarling Scott as Johnny helped him haul the cowboy back to his feet.

The bullet which had passed straight through the fleshy part of his left arm was long gone. Blood poured from the raw, open wound as the rancher tore off his bandanna and wrapped it tightly above the injury.

'Who in tarnation you bin shooting at, Kelso?' Adams asked as he knotted the fabric.

'Skinner,' Scott answered. 'Who else would I be shooting at out here in the middle of the street?'

'It couldn't have bin Skinner,' Johnny said as he supported the shaking wrangler.

'It sure was! I nearly had him too!' Scott raged waving his gun at the hotel. 'I nearly made me a thousand bucks!'

'But we just had us a confab with Skinner down outside the marshal's office, boy,' Adams insisted. 'There ain't no way on this earth that he could have gotten up here in time for you to have a showdown with him.'

Scott's expression altered. 'It was him, I tell you! I recognized the black leather gear he wears. He come out of that alley and stepped up on to the boardwalk just as I come round from over yonder. I called him out and he went for his gun but I was faster. He plugged me but I reckon I winged him as well. He weren't as fast as I thought he'd be.'

'That don't make no sense, Gene,' Johnny said to the stony-faced rancher. 'There ain't no way Kelso could outdraw Skinner!'

'It weren't Skinner, Johnny,' Adams drawled. 'We know it couldn't have bin him.'

'It sure was!' Scott protested.

'Did you see his face?' Adams pressed. 'Hear his voice?'

'No, but he was wearing the same leather gear he was wearing when he killed Clu,' Scott muttered. He was starting to feel the effects of the loss of blood from his arm. 'I ain't seen nobody else in Death who dresses like that. Have you?'

'This lad's had himself a leetle bit too much sun, Gene boy,' Tomahawk said, nodding as he made a circling gesture with his finger beside his own head. 'Fried his brain.'

Adams glanced at his oldest pal in amazement. 'You might not have noticed but it's the middle of the night, you old fool. The sun went down hours back.'

'It's like sunburn, Gene boy. Takes a while to sizzle. Yep, I figure Kelso's brain is like a fried egg inside that skull of his.' Tomahawk shrugged, then he spotted the door of the doctor's office open and the familiar sight of Don Harper emerge. 'Say! There's Don!'

Adams and Johnny turned the bleeding cowboy and walked with him to where the lawman stood. Tomahawk lingered outside the well-lit hotel and rubbed his bushy beard thoughtfully. He walked to the steps, then paused. A well-suited man poked his head round the open door frame and stared at the old-timer. Marve Johnson was a small and cowardly man who had somehow found himself in the West when every ounce of him longed to be back East where he had been born and raised.

'Has the shooting stopped?'

Tomahawk walked up the steps. He stopped and stared at the wooden boards close to where the man lurked. A few droplets of blood sparkled in the amber lights. Scott had been right, he thought. He had winged the man he thought was Skinner.

'You see who leaked that blood, *amigo*?' Tomahawk asked the petrified Johnson.

The man looked down and then went pale. 'Oh dear! Blood! Blood on my porch! I ask you, what sort of greeting is that to paying guests? You spend a fortune on imported drapes and wallpaper and then someone starts to bleed on it! It's too much!'

Tomahawk circled around the blood. He was careful not to step in it as he closed in on the man.

'I asked you if you seen who got themselves shot by here, mister. I ain't troubled about your damn drapes and suchlike.'

Johnson blinked hard and attempted to compose himself. 'I did not! When the shooting started I took cover down behind my desk in there!'

'That figures! I didn't take you to be the brave type!' Tomahawk raised his bushy eyebrows. 'Now, think on. Did you see a varmint dressed in black leather?'

117

'Mr Skinner dresses in that fashion,' the man replied. 'I think it suits certain sorts.'

'Skinner?' Tomahawk rolled his eyes as his tongue rotated around his toothless mouth. 'But he's down at the other end of town!'

'He might well be but he's the only man I know who dresses like that.' The man straightened up. 'I shall have to have my boy wash that down before it dries.'

'You got a son?' Tomahawk could not hide his shock.

Johnson looked heavenward. 'No! I mean the boy that works for me as a porter. I'm not married.'

'Figures.'

'Will you please leave now?' Johnson waved his hand at the old cowpoke. 'This has been rather upsetting.'

Tomahawk scratched his beard again. 'My pal Kelso said that a man dressed all in black leather was standing right here a few minutes back. You sure you didn't see him?'

'Wait a minute!' The man's expression changed. It was as if his memory had suddenly returned to him after the shock of the shoot-out on his porch. 'I do recall seeing Mr Skinner standing there a minute or so before the shooting began. He had his back to me but it was him, OK.'

'You sure it was him?'

'My fragrant friend, I saw him!' Johnson insisted.

'Where'd he go?' Tomahawk could not understand how one man could be in two different places at the same time. 'Up to his room?'

The man suddenly looked blank. 'Actually I don't know where he went. Like I told you, I ducked down behind the desk. Is it really that important?'

'Damned if I know.' Tomahawk started walking towards the doctor's office and the forlorn-looking men who were waiting outside its weathered façade.

Adams watched as Tomahawk came towards them. 'Ben's dead!'

Tomahawk screwed up his face. For a while he did not speak as he rested his ancient bones down on the boardwalk. He stared out at the still busy street where the sound of many out-of-tune pianos filled the night air. Along the thoroughfare the Wells Fargo boys had hooked up six fresh horses to the stagecoach in readiness for the next leg of its journey. His wrinkled eyes watched as both guard and driver clambered up on to the high seat then drove down the dusty street until they had left the town. When they had disappeared Tomahawk turned his head and stared at the three grim faces above him.

'You figure Skinner got himself a twin?' he asked.

All three men looked down at Tomahawk. The question was not as strange as it at first sounded. Adams sat on the edge of a hitching rail and leaned over his friend.

'Where's that fuzzy old brain of yours going with questions like that, Tomahawk? Do you know something that the rest of us don't?'

Tomahawk nodded for a few moments. 'I was chatting with a real fancy man up at the hotel. I figure he owns the place. Anyways, he was saying that he saw Skinner outside his hotel just before the shooting started.'

Johnny crouched down. 'He couldn't have!'

'We saw Skinner outside Don's office only seconds before the shooting started,' Adams said with a sigh. 'A man can't be in two places at the same time.'

Harper stepped down from the boardwalk and stood directly before the brooding old man.

'But you say that Johnson, the hotel owner, said he saw Skinner there?'

Tomahawk nodded. 'Leastways, he saw an *hombre* wearing black leather from hat to toe! That's why I was wondering if there was two Skinners in Death.'

Adams rose to his full height. His eyes looked down the long street to the marshal's office and then back to the hotel. Then he started to nod exactly as Tomahawk was doing.

'Skinner showed me his guns!' Adams said. 'He made a little fuss about it but that was play-acting. He was waiting outside the office to prove he wasn't the man who gunned down Clevis and Ben. But why?'

120

'You reckon he got a partner?' Harper asked.

'Another locobean!' Tomahawk sniffed. 'Two mindless killers just trying to send us off in all directions so we end up catching nothing but our own tails.'

Harper closed in on Adams. Their eyes locked on to one another's.

'What's this all about, Gene? Can you figure it?' There was a tone in the lawman's voice which hinted at pleading. The man was desperate for answers. Answers which none of them was able to offer. 'I lost me two fine boys and you've had one of yours killed and the other hurt real bad. What is this all about?'

Adams raised a hand and placed it on the marshal's shoulder.

'This ain't the work of no locobean, Don. There's purpose behind this slaughter and I'm gonna try and find out what it is.'

'Purpose?' Harper repeated. 'Killing for the sake of killing can't ever have no purpose that I can figure.'

'But it has!' Adams was convinced of it. 'I'm certain that there must be a reason behind the killings.'

Johnny checked his guns. 'We still bound by the law, Don?'

Harper nodded. 'We have to be, Johnny. Without

the law there ain't nothing but more of this kinda thing.'

Adams checked his own guns, then started to reload them with bullets from his belt.

'There's still a long while before midnight and a handful of hours of darkness after that until sunup, boys. I'm gonna start looking.'

'Looking for what, Gene?' Harper asked.

'Answers!' Adams retorted.

FOURTEEN

The four men had decided that if they were to have any chance of catching the killer with a smoking gun in his hand they had better separate. Harper had gone south of Main Street whilst Johnny Puma had ventured towards the west, where the livery stable towered over most of the other ramshackle buildings in the area. Tomahawk had decided to try his luck at the eastern end of Death as Adams headed north. The odds were against any of them even setting eyes upon the killer they sought before he ruthlessly struck again. All any of them knew for sure was that there was another man who dressed exactly like Skinner somewhere in the streets and alleys of Death.

But was he the man who had slain both of Harper's deputies?

Things were getting tense.

Reaching a street-lantern perched high on a pole, Adams pulled his golden hunter from his pocket and flipped open its lid. The flickering illumination from the lantern danced off the glass of the timepiece as the rancher studied it. It was now getting close to eleven and the tall man had walked more than two miles from the very centre of the town called Death.

He snapped the lid shut and dropped the watch back into his pocket. This was the part of town where the monied people gathered. The houses here were big and, unlike the majority of the others in this settlement, stood apart from one another in their own grounds.

Adams rubbed a thumb across his jaw.

There were no brothels, saloons or gambling-houses here, he thought. Folks here pretended to be above such base desires although he knew that probably all of the menfolk who lived in this area spent more time and money in those establishments than other less wealthy people.

The rancher was about to turn and head back towards the heart of Death when he heard a horse thundering along the tree-lined street. Adams stepped back until he was beside a large rambling bush. He wanted to see but to be unseen.

The rider drove his mount over the crest of a hill which stood between here and the rest of town. As the horseman spurred his horse on he passed beneath the streetlight which Adams himself had used to see the hands of his timepiece with.

It looked like Skinner.

Exactly like Skinner.

But was it him?

The question burned into the rancher's mind as the horse galloped on towards the wealthiest part of town. Adams stepped back on to the road and rubbed his neck thoughtfully. He knew that all he had really seen was the leather garb the rider was dressed in. No light had reached the face beneath the wide brim of the horseman's Stetson.

Adams's thoughts returned to the events earlier when Chuck Foyle had been shot. Foyle and every other member of the Cattlemen's Association lived in this area, he told himself.

Could it have been Skinner who had killed Foyle? The deadly accurate bullet had been the same as the ones which had dispatched both Clu Brooks and Dan Cooper.

The rancher knew that Skinner had probably not killed the pair of deputies or winged Kelso Scott because Skinner was a marksman. Again the troubled rancher wondered whether he ought to continue his walk to see where the rider had gone. He cursed himself for not getting his horse from the livery. This terrain was not meant to be walked by men in high-heeled boots.

Again the troublesome question burned into his mind like a branding-iron.

Had Skinner killed Foyle?

If so, perhaps the gunman was going to try and kill another member of the association. Before Adams had time to ponder the possible motives behind such actions he heard the sound of a single-horse buggy coming from the same direction as the rider had used. He turned and remained exactly where he was. This time he did not care whether the driver of the vehicle saw him or not.

The buggy came hurtling over the crest and travelled along the otherwise empty street at speed. Adams stood back and watched as the man drove the horse on at breakneck pace. The cracking of the whip stung the air as the driver urged the animal on.

This time there was no mistaking the man in the buggy. Adams knew there was only one person that big in Death.

'Coltrane!' Adams breathed to himself.

The buggy continued up over the hill to where even bigger dwellings stood in even larger grounds. The rancher rubbed his chin and bit his lip.

Coltrane had looked scared.

Damn scared.

Perhaps, after seeing one of his partners gunned down, the man had suddenly become aware of his own mortality. Even though the buggy was now out of sight the sound of Coltrane's whip could still be heard.

Adams paused for a moment and pulled the collar of his jacket up until it protected his neck. His eyes gazed upward at the steep mountainside. There was an eerie mist descending now from the trees.

The light of the moon was already becoming fainter as the fog drifted across the wealthier part of town. Adams did not like mist at the best of times. He liked to see things clearly and not have his vision hampered.

The rancher was thoughtful.

So far the killer or killers had struck either in or from the safety of the town's alleys. Even Chuck Foyle had been shot from the end of an alley. So far the killer had been protected by shadows in the heart of the town.

Would he have the guts to step out from those shadows to this far more open place? Adams thought about the horseman who had thundered past him only moments earlier. Whether it was Skinner or his murderous lookalike made no difference. The rider had gone in the same direction taken by Coltrane.

To Adams that meant only one thing: that Coltrane might be headed towards his own destruction.

Bright lights from hundreds of lamps and lanterns twinkled in the frosty night air down in the busy town but even though they lured a myriad moths and countless defiant men who refused to accept the passage of time and sleep when nature told them to do so, Adams turned his back on them.

The rancher headed on to where he had seen both rider and buggy driver heading. He tried to increase his pace but high-heeled boots were not designed to walk in. They were meant to slide into stirrups.

Defiantly refusing to acknowledge the fact that his feet hurt, Gene Adams pressed on through the swirling damp fog.

He rested his hands on the grips of his holstered guns as his long strides ate up the ground. The gnawing in his craw warned him that he was going to have to use his guns before the night got much older.

Adams was ready.

Cyril Coltrane had driven his buggy to his home with a heart that pounded like an Apache war drum. He was scared and it showed. Sweat ran down his face and belied the chill that engulfed the area as the fog grew thicker. Coltrane had heard the earlier gunfire and left Parker, Quinn and Fuller back in their private room in the Diamond Pin playing poker. Reflecting on Foyle's murder had brought it home to the large man that no amount of money could protect you from an assassin's bullet.

His magnificent house was set in an acre of well-maintained grounds and let everyone know that he was rich. Far richer than anyone else in the town. Until this moment he had rejoiced in the fact but now wondered if it might be his and his partners' wealth that had something to do with Foyle's being murdered. He and his partners did not dwell in dust-caked ranch houses out on the range but chose to live in luxury in Death.

The buggy slowed as Coltrane drew back on the reins and stopped the lathered-up horse beside the white picket fence. He saw one of his servants appear from the large house and rush towards him.

The handsome building was, like all the others in the wealthy area of the town constructed from the plentiful supply timber that flanked the settlement on both sides. Yet his home was different from the majority. It was solid and designed to display its owner's obvious prosperity.

Yet this night the large man wished that he and it were totally invisible. As he stepped down from the buggy and handed the reins to the servant, Coltrane suddenly felt a chill run down his spine.

Fear was something which, until earlier, he had never truly experienced. That had all changed when he had seen Chuck Foyle killed right next to him. Coltrane wondered whether the bullet had been meant for Foyle or was really intended for him.

129

The thought terrified him.

No matter how hard he tried he could not get the image of his dead partner lying in a pool of blood from his mind.

A stiff breeze cut across the grounds. Branches of trees swayed like drunken cowhands but did not seem to have any effect on the fog which now thickened. Shadows were everywhere. Shadows that Coltrane could not recall ever noticing before. He was now really scared. It was like a cancer. It was consuming him and he was helpless to do anything about it.

He glanced at his servant. The man led the horse and buggy round the corner of his house towards the stables at the rear of the building.

Coltrane walked towards the front door of his luxurious home. A light above the door beckoned him. Yet every step was like walking in quicksand.

As the breeze intensified Coltrane's eyes darted at every movement in the garden. He felt sick and yet no matter how he tried he could not walk any faster. Then a noise to his right drew his attention. There was no mistaking the sound a dried branch made when snapped beneath the boot of a man. A man who lay in wait.

Coltrane froze.

He could no longer take another step. He turned and stared in the direction from where he had heard the sound. His heart felt as though it was going to explode. Then he saw the figure through the thickening fog. Trey Skinner was walking straight towards him. Coltrane clawed at the holstered .44 he always wore on his hip.

His clammy hand drew the gun. He raised it and aimed.

'Who is it?' Coltrane stammered. 'Who are you? What do you want here?'

'Mr Coltrane?' Skinner stopped walking. He glared at the cattleman with fiery eyes as fog swirled about his form.

Coltrane felt his throat go dry. It was as though a noose had been tightened beneath his many chins.

'Who are you?' Coltrane managed to ask once more.

'Why, I'm the man that's gonna kill you!' Skinner smiled as he saw the gun in the cattleman's shaking hand.

'What?' Coltrane gulped.

'You heard me, fatman.'

'There must be a mistake.'

'Draw!' Skinner knew that men like Coltrane were just as easy to kill as had been the hapless cowboy in the Broken Bottle. For men who seldom used their weaponry nearly always forgot that most guns required their hammers to be locked into position before their triggers could be used.

Frantically, Coltrane's fat finger kept pulling at the trigger but nothing happened. Only when Coltrane realized his mistake and tried to drag the hammer back with his thumb did he see Skinner move.

The gunman drew and fanned his hammer once. The single shot rang out around the area as the hot missile of lethal lead tore into Coltrane's chest with the force of a mule kick.

The large man staggered backward with unblinking eyes. He felt the gun drop from his hand and then hit the ground. A gasp of air rattled from the open mouth as blood suddenly exposed the expertly placed bullet hole in the handmade shirt.

Coltrane was dead.

'Now the rest!' Skinner laughed. He blew the smoke from the barrel of his gun, holstered the weapon, turned and ran to the picket fence. He leapt over it, dragged his reins free and threw himself on to his saddle.

As Skinner steadied the horse he could hear hysterical voices raised inside the house. He knew it was time to go and swung the animal around.

He spurred and galloped out on to the street just as Gene Adams came into view. The rancher stopped the rider whipped his mount with the tails of his reins and headed straight for him. Adams saw Skinner's gun appear from its holster. He leapt into the bushes at the side of the street just as a bullet was fired.

The bullet took a chunk of bark off a tree next to the rancher. Red-hot splinters showered over Adams as he dragged one of his own guns from its holster.

Adams clambered back to his feet and fired.

But it was too late. Skinner had disappeared into the bank of dense fog. The tall rancher listened to the sound of the horse's hoofs as they headed back into the heart of town. Then another, more chilling sound drew his attention.

It was the wailing of Coltrane's widow.

The rancher brushed himself down and rushed to the sound of the grieving female. He reached the white picket fence within a minute. He slowed as he approached the kneeling woman and the servants who flanked both her and the body.

Adams walked to them and looked down in horror at Cyril Coltrane's body, The face of the cattleman's widow glanced up at the rancher, whom she had met on several occasions.

'Who would do this, Gene?' Her voice begged for answers.

Adams respectfully removed his black hat and shook his head. He placed a hand on her shoulder.

'Can you lend me a horse, ma'am?' he asked. 'I saw the killer on his way back into town! He took a shot at me as well, but I was a tad luckier than Cyril!'

The female looked up to one of her servants. 'Get Mr Adams a horse, Joshua!'

133

'Right away, Mrs Coltrane!' The servant nodded.

'Thank you, ma'am!' Adams returned his hat to his head.

'Get him, Gene!' she said. 'Make him pay!'

'I'll surely try,' Adams drawled.

'Come with me, sir!' Joshua said. The servant ran, with Adams keeping pace with him at his shoulder, towards the stables.

FIFTEEN

Johnny Puma had just rounded the corner on his way back towards Main Street when his sharp eyes caught a brief glimpse of a horseman who was whipping his mount furiously as he came back into the very heart of the town. The cowboy ran to the corner of the Silver Dollar gambling house and pushed his way through the crowd of drunken men who had gathered upon its well-illuminated porch. As the rider flashed past the building he dragged rein and violently turned his mount into a dark side-street. Upon reaching the narrower street, where the dust from the animal's hoofs still hung in the air, Johnny knew that he had just seen one of the men who wore black leather trail gear. The youngster screwed up his eyes but the horseman had already disappeared from view. The fog that had come down from the mountainside now was drifting like a plague of phantoms through the rows of wooden buildings.

Johnny pulled the leather safety loops off his gun hammers and began to run in pursuit of the rider.

Skinner reined in behind the Diamond Pin and studied the building with well-informed eyes. He dipped the fingers of his left hand into his vest pocket and withdrew a scrap of paper. He studied the hand-drawn markings carefully, then returned it to the pocket. With one fluid action he dismounted, tied his reins to a tree branch and then climbed through a gaping hole in the fence before him. The rear of the building appeared to be as secure as any bank but the scrap of paper had told the gunman differently. Skinner walked through the bare yard to an oak door. The door seemed to be impenetrable, and it was to those who did not have the information Skinner had.

The man did not go for the lock but its hinges. Hinges which were well greased and had been loosened. Skinner smiled. He pulled a penknife from his pants pocket and opened up its well-used blade. In a matter of seconds both hinges had been prised from the body of the door.

He cast them aside and then poked the blade into the narrow gap between the frame and the solid door. He levered it several times until it came towards him in one piece. Skinner placed the knife between his teeth, gripped both sides of the door and pulled it free of the frame.

He rested the large object against the rear wall of the gambling house and entered. Without missing a step he folded the knife and returned it to his pocket. No light entered the hall that he was walking down yet he knew exactly where he was heading.

Twelve paces into the darkness, Skinner stopped.

He pictured the crude map that he had just read, then turned to his left and reached out with both hands. Another door greeted his gloved fingers. Exactly as the map had indicated.

Skinner ran his hands around the frame until he found the key he had been told would be there. Carefully he brought the key down, then he found a stout lock. The key slid into the hole and he turned it slowly.

A clicking sound filled his ears.

Skinner smiled even more widely.

Using both hands against the door, he eased it back. There was no sound. This door had been greased just as the outer one had. Skinner pressed his face up against the gap and stared into what appeared to be a small room. Buckets and mops were next to a wall. A wall from which a staircase rose.

Skinner opened the door fully and walked confidently into the room. This was also exactly as it had been shown on the scrap of paper he carried. Every detail had been marked in pencil so that the ruthless Skinner would not be able to make a false move.

The gunman walked to the bottom of the steps and looked up to where a small window allowed moonlight to enter. The staircase turned as though it had been built to hug the outer wall perfectly. Skinner knew that this was not a place any of the patrons of the gambling house would ever see. This was for the people who cleaned the well-appointed building to move freely from one level to the next without ever being witnessed. For wealthy people do not like to see those who do their cleaning for them.

Out of sight and out of mind.

The gunman began to ascend the steps. The sound of men's voices came from above him. Every step that Skinner took made him twist and turn his head in order to ensure that there were no others in this dark place.

But there were no others in the confines of this dark place. He was alone.

There was only one door at the top of the staircase. He knew that this door allowed the lesser mortals access to the private room whilst its privileged members would use one which went out through the building's more splendid surroundings. Skinner reached the top of the steps and stood on a small landing no more than four feet square.

It was enough, though.

He moved a shoulder and allowed the moonlight from the window to shine fully on the door before him. The key was in its lock, as he knew it would be.

Again he smiled.

The private room of the Diamond Pin was filled with cigar smoke as three men rose from the gaming-table and had one last drink. They had tried to ignore the brutal events of the evening but none had managed to do so.

'You figuring on going home or staying at the hotel?' Quinn asked the other two men.

'The hotel might be a little safer, Brad,' Fuller said as he stacked the dozens of coloured chips together in the centre of the table. 'That killer might be out there waiting for us right now. If he killed Chuck then none of us is safe!'

'Coltrane had the right idea.'

Parker looked as though he had been pistol-whipped. Terror was something which had grown inside him and no amount of hard liquor had been able to douse its flames. Sweat had already soaked his shirt as well as his tailored top coat, but he refused to admit the obvious to his partners.

'My horse is out front,' he said. 'I'm going home and no gun-toting bastard can stop me.'

Quinn eyed Parker. 'Well, I'm scared of that long journey back home, Pete, and I don't care who knows it.'

Then without warning the three cattlemen heard the unexpected sound of the key in its lock.

They turned and stared at the door which they had only ever seen opened when the gambling house staff discreetly brought them extra supplies of whiskey.

The ruthless Trey Skinner was not bringing them anything but death. He took one step into the room and gave out a long sigh as his right hand hovered above the holstered .45.

'What in tarnation?' Quinn gasped.

Fuller narrowed his eyes. 'Who is it?'

Fearfully, Parker dropped his glass. Its contents spilled out across the floor.

'Oh my God!'

'Reckon you'll be meeting him real soon, mister!' Skinner smiled. Then faster than any of them could have imagined possible, he drew the gun from his right hip and fanned its hammer three times with his gloved left hand.

Each moment was lethal. Each bullet was perfectly placed in the stunned men's hearts.

Quinn, Parker and Fuller were knocked off their feet and thrown across the floor. Trails of gruesome gore marked their trail to where they landed.

The gunman raised the Colt and blew down its smoking barrel before opening the weapon and allowing the hot casings to fall on to the floor covering.

His fingers swiftly reloaded the gun before it was spun back into its holster.

'Much obliged, gentlemen!' The smiling Skinner touched the brim of his hat, stepped back and then closed the door again. He locked it and made his way down the stairs.

Out in the street scores of people stared at the Diamond Pin as even more of its patrons and staff emerged from the brightly lit building. The sound of the three deadly shots had rung out through its walls and caused a panicked evacuation just as Gene Adams galloped down Main Street towards it.

Johnny Puma saw the rancher and flagged him down with his hat. The young cowboy watched as the big man pulled back on his reins and dropped down to the sand.

'Where'd them shots come from, Johnny?' Adams asked as he held on to the reins.

'Inside the Diamond Pin.'

Adams gave a knowing nod. 'Reckon I know who the targets were.'

Johnny was just about to speak when the owner of the gambling hall pushed his way through the crowd to Adams. Sly Harvey was not usually a man who showed any emotion but even he could not disguise the concern that had gripped him.

'Gene!' Harvey gasped. 'Three of my members have bin gunned down upstairs! I just found them!'

141

'They wouldn't happen to be Fuller, Quinn and Parker?' Adams asked as he studied the reins in his hands. 'Would they?'

Harvey nodded in amazement. 'Yeah! How'd you figure that?'

The rancher did not reply. He turned to Johnny and handed the cowboy the reins to his borrowed horse. 'Go find Tomahawk, boy! We got us some tracking to do and he's the only man I know who got the skill.'

Johnny threw himself on top of the horse and spurred.

SIXTEEN

With a steely glare, Gene Adams watched as Johnny and Tomahawk rode towards him with the rancher's chestnut mare in tow. Just as the cowboys reined in outside the gambling hall Adams saw the figure of Marshal Harper emerge from his office and step down to his own tethered horse. The lawman pulled the reins free of the hitching rail and swung the animal round. Harper held on to the saddle horn, pushed his left boot into the stirrup and hoisted himself up atop his sixteen-hand gelding. He tapped his spurs and rode down the street to where Adams and his men awaited.

'Tomahawk here is gonna track the varmint who killed Foyle and the others,' Adams announced as he mounted his tall chestnut mare and steadied it.

'Leastways old Coltrane had the brains to light out for home earlier!' Harper said. He placed the stem

143

of his unlit pipe between his teeth.

Adams looked straight at the lawman. 'Coltrane's as dead as the others, Don.'

'What?' Harper gasped.

'He was gunned down outside his house,' Adams added. 'His widow begged me to catch his killer.'

The marshal edged his horse closer to the stony-faced rancher. 'Did you see who done it?'

'Yep,' Adams confirmed with a nod. 'It was Skinner. I didn't see his face but I seen the bullet hole in Cyril's chest. The same as the ones that killed my boy Clu and the others. Only Skinner can shoot that well!'

Harper nodded slowly. 'Yeah! My boys were cut to ribbons by someone who relied on quantity of lead rather than quality of markmaship.'

The rancher turned and looked at Tomahawk. 'Get tracking, older timer. We got us a killer to catch.'

Tomahawk touched his battered hat brim. 'That varmint's already caught, Gene boy!'

A myriad stars competed with the bright moon above the unscrupulous horseman as he thundered out of Death. A massive boulder stood more than thirty feet high ahead of him, indicating where the town ended and the fertile range began. Skinner leaned back and dug his boots into his stirrups to slow the horse beneath him. A signpost stood between his snorting mount and the massive chunk of rock.

Skinner stopped the animal under him, leaned across and rested his left hand on the top of the marker. He screwed up his eyes and read the single word painted upon it.

'Death!' he said. A smile crossed his features.

He steadied his horse and looked all around him for a few moments. This was the place he had been instructed to come to by the man who had hired his deadly talents. The gunman opened the cover of his timepiece and looked at its face for a few moments.

It was nearly midnight and he had achieved all of the tasks he had been set. He was ahead of schedule, but he knew that that would not earn him any bonus.

Suddenly Skinner's keen senses alerted him. His right hand instinctively went to the grip of his holstered weapon. Then he saw a shadow trace across the sand behind the boulder. It was the shadow of a horse and its rider.

'I know you're there, Foyle!' Skinner called out.

The horseman appeared from the cover of the rock and guided his mount to where Skinner waited. Skinner looked at the black leather trail gear that Bud Foyle wore and grinned wide. It was exactly the same as the clothing he himself sported. Both outfits had been purchased by the rider who now approached.

'Well?' Chuck Foyle's son asked as he stopped his mount close to the gunman's. 'Is it finished?'

Skinner smiled. 'Yep! They're all dead just like you wanted, Bud.'

Foyle dismounted and wrapped his reins around the signpost. Then he walked to where he could see the sprawling town spread out before him. Skinner threw his right leg over the neck of his mount and slid to the ground.

Both men studied one another. They were almost mirror images when clad in the same clothes. Only the cruel smile which etched the gunman's features was different. Bud Foyle did not seem ever to alter his callow expression.

'I did my bit! I sure gave those deputies a bad time!' Foyle boasted. 'Reckon that took the pressure off your back for a while, Skinner!'

Skinner nodded as he too looped his reins around the post and knotted the long leathers. 'You're right. Sure confused them stinking cowpokes who bin helping that dumb marshal. Reckon they'll never be able to figure out how one man could be in two different places at the same time.'

'My plan for you and me to wear the same gear really mixed them critters up.' Foyle sighed as he moved to his saddle-bags and opened the nearest satchel.

Skinner watched as Foyle pulled out a bulging bag

and handed it to him. The sound of coins pleased him.

'Here's your blood-money!' Foyle said.

'It better all be here, *amigo*!' Skinner loosened the drawstring and stared at the gold coins before he strode to his own horse. He flicked the buckle of his own saddlebag satchel and pushed the bag of coins into it. 'Tell me something, Foyle!'

'What?'

'I can understand you wanting them cattlemen killed but why did you have me kill your own father?' Skinner circled Foyle.

'Why?' Foyle raised an eyebrow.

Skinner nodded. 'Yeah. Why?'

'Because they were all business partners, Skinner. With them all dead I have complete control of the Cattlemen's Association,' Foyle said. 'My pa had to die just like the others.'

The gunman paused. His eyes narrowed. 'Ain't them other men got no kin?'

'They have but I'm the only one of legal age to take over the business,' Foyle answered smugly. 'You see, their wives ain't got no legal rights in law. Businesses are owned and run by men. Men over the age of twenty-one.'

Skinner frowned. 'Kinda cold-hearted to pay someone to kill your own pa though, ain't it?'

Foyle looked angry. 'He was a womanizer and a

drunk. He ain't no loss to anyone!'

'That makes what I gotta do a damn sight easier!' The gunman squared up to Foyle. His fingers were twitching above the grip of his right-hand gun. 'Killing you will be a real pleasure!'

Suddenly Bud Foyle realized that the man he had hired to kill so many others was actually serious. He felt his heart quicken as he stared across the moonlit distance between them into the smiling face. The face that so many others had seen just before Skinner dispatched them to boot hill.

'What in tarnation are you saying, Skinner?' Foyle protested. 'I've paid you and that's it.'

'That ain't it at all!'

Foyle's jaw dropped. 'Why kill me?'

'Because you know who I am, Bud,' Skinner said through gritted teeth. 'I gotta kill you so that nobody else finds out the truth. With you dead dressed like that I reckon nobody will give me a second thought. I'll ride south and enjoy them golden eagles.'

Foyle took a step forward. 'Do you want more money? I'll get you more money! Just name the amount and I'll get it for you!'

The gunman inhaled deeply. 'Draw!'

Foyle looked to both sides of him. There was nowhere to hide. The massive boulder was ten feet behind him. Sweat began to run down his face as his cruel mind raced in desperation. This was not what he had planned. This was not part of the deal.

'I-I ain't no gunslinger!'

'Draw!' Skinner repeated.

Foyle had run out of ideas. He went for both his holstered guns and managed to drag them from their holsters at a speed which amazed even him.

But Trey Skinner was faster.

Far faster.

In one deadly action Skinner drew and fanned his gun hammer. The solitary blast of explosive venom erupted from the barrel of the Colt. For a brief second the gunman could see the startled eyes of his victim. The shot hit Foyle high and knocked him off his feet. The spoiled son of a wealthy cattleman went flying backwards and crashed into the boulder. But he was not dead. Foyle clawed both hammers back and managed to squeeze his triggers. Two shots kicked up the sand to either side of him as the approaching gunman closed in to finish his handiwork.

Skinner looked down at the man who bled like a stuck pig from the bullet hole in his neck. There was no mercy, only the unholy smile of a man who always bettered those less capable.

'First time today I missed what I was aiming at, Bud,' the gunman admitted. 'I reckon that must really hurt!'

The mortally wounded Foyle spluttered but no

149

words came from his mouth. Only crimson gore. It ran down his chin like a river. His eyes widened when he saw the face of the lethal Skinner smile down at him.

With merciless precision, Skinner fanned his gun hammer again.

This time the shot was deadly accurate and went straight into the heart of the man on the ground. Foyle buckled and then fell limp. Skinner blew down the barrel of his gun, replaced the two spent bullets with fresh ones from his belt and smiled.

But the smile was short-lived.

As he turned to walk to his horse he heard a sound.

It was the sound of riders heading his way.

Trey Skinner lowered his head and stared hard. Then he saw them.

The four horsemen drove their mounts through the low mist and on towards him. They looked like ghosts to the onlooker. Although Skinner did not know it, the expert tracker Tomahawk had found his trail behind the Diamond Pin and led his companions out of town to this place.

'Damn it all!' Skinner cursed as he grabbed his saddle horn and swung up on top of his horse. He glanced around the range and knew that it held no cover. The gunman hauled his reins hard to his left, steadied his mount and stared at the moonlit image of Death far behind the riders.

A thought came to him. If he circled widely through the rocks he knew that he could get back into the town and then lie in wait for his hunters.

Skinner drove his spurs into the flesh of his horse. It responded and thundered away from the dead body of Bud Foyle as its master hung low against its neck, watching those he prayed could not see him.

But the moon betrayed him.

Skinner had not even covered a quarter-mile when he heard the raised voices of his pursuers. They had spotted him and changed direction quickly.

They were now hot on his heels.

FINALE

Kelso Scott stood on the porch outside the doctor's office with his arm in a sling. He pulled a twisted cigar remnant from his shirt pocket and placed it between his teeth. He found a match and ran it down the wooden upright. He drew on its flame. As his lungs filled with smoke he caught a fleeting glimpse of Skinner as the gunman thundered into Main Street before turning his exhausted mount and spurring it on into a side-street opposite him.

Although the town was still busy with many horsemen there was no way that the wrangler could or would ever forget the sight of the man in leather.

'It's him!'

Scott dragged more smoke into his lungs, then stepped down from the boardwalk and hurried across Main Street. He reached the corner of the Red Branch saloon and stared down into the long winding street. Only one lantern burned down there but its light was enough.

The wrangler watched as Skinner dismounted quickly and then pulled his hefty bags from the saddle cantle. After observing the gunman enter an apparently empty house halfway along the street, Scott dropped the cigar on to the ground and crushed it with his boot.

His good arm rested its hand on his gun grip.

He was about to advance blindly when he heard the hoofs of galloping riders behind him. Scott turned and looked at Adams and his three companions astride their trusty mounts, heading towards him. Oblivious to any possible risk, Scott stepped out into the street and stopped the four horsemen in their tracks.

Adams held his reins up to his chin and glared at the wrangler angrily. 'You tired of living, Kelso?'

'What you doing, boy?' Harper shouted.

Johnny leapt from his pinto and ran up to his pal. 'What you doing out here, Kelso?'

Scott turned and looked down the side street. 'Skinner! He's down there! I seen him!'

Tomahawk nodded knowingly. 'I knew that already. Tracks never lie, not like the varmints that make 'em!'

Marshal Harper got down from his high-shouldered gelding and tossed his reins aside. He

153

marched up to Kelso, who still had his arm in a sling, and peered down into the dimly lit street. 'Down there? Are you sure?'

'Damn right I am,' Scott insisted. 'See that horse? That's his and when he left it he was carrying a mighty heavy-looking saddle-bag, Marshal.'

Adams dropped to the ground. 'Where'd he go?'

'See the building with the beaten-up door?' Scott asked them. 'He ran in there.'

Adams stood beside Harper. 'What is that building, Don?'

'Just an empty house, Gene,' the lawman answered. 'Used to be a whorehouse before the cholera a few years back. Half the folks along this street died. Nobody wants to live down there.'

'Bad wells, I'll bet you!' Tomahawk sniffed. 'Bad wells kills more people than Apaches!'

Adams checked his guns. Then he looked at the marshal. 'Does that house have a back door leading someplace else?'

Harper pondered the question, then snapped his fingers when the answer came to him. 'It sure does! And that leads to the Silver Dollar gambling place.'

The rancher looked at Johnny, then Tomahawk. He raised a finger to the youngster.

'You and Tomahawk wait here. If Skinner comes back out of there I want you two to make sure he don't escape.'

154

Johnny looked at Harper. 'Can we shoot the bastard?'

Harper nodded. 'Tell him to give himself up first.' If he goes for his guns I give you licence to finish him.'

'What about me?' Scott moved between the lawman and the rancher. He was still nursing his arm. 'I got me a good reason to dislike that critter more than any of you.'

Adams raised an eyebrow. 'You can help Tomahawk and Johnny, Kelso.'

Harper looked at Adams. 'What we gonna do?'

'We're going to the Silver Dollar, Don!' Adams had barely finished his sentence before he started to run along the boardwalk in the direction of the gambling hall.

Although he was carrying a lot of weight Harper managed to keep up with the far fitter rancher. Both men arrived outside the tall building at the same moment and entered.

The gambling house was nearly empty. Half a dozen men at two tables tables still played poker as Adams and the marshal walked swiftly into the main room. To their surprise Skinner was seated at the far wall with his bulging saddle-bags on the green baize table before him. Neither man could see his hands as they strode towards him.

'Got you!' Harper said angrily.

Skinner kept his hands hidden. 'What have I done?'

Realizing the possible peril, Adams stopped his friend's advance. Both stood fifteen feet away from the gunman as the gamblers realized the imminent danger and hastily started to leave the room and the building.

Harper looked to Adams. Although he did not speak his expression was asking the taller man why he had prevented them from continuing on towards the seated figure.

'You done a lot of killing today, Skinner,' Adams drawled. He rested his hands on his hips and stared at the gunman. 'We're here to put a stop to it!'

Skinner smiled. 'I figure you gotta have proof of that even in a town like this! You got any proof?'

Adams smiled back at Skinner. 'Me and the marshal have decided to forget about needing proof, sonny. You killed them men and you're gonna pay.'

For the first time since he had reached this remote town, Skinner was troubled. He licked his lips. They were dry. He cleared his throat.

'You can't do that! It ain't legal!'

Gene Adams took a step closer to the table and tilted his head. His smile was now burning into the seated man, sapping the gunman's confidence.

'We don't give a damn, Skinner!' Adams looked around the large room. 'There ain't nobody here except us three. We kill you and tell the folks out there in the street that you started it and they'll believe us.'

Skinner was now ashen-faced. He listened to the words from the tall man and knew that Adams meant each and every one of them. He had never squared up to anyone who might have had a chance of matching his gun skills. The rancher looked as though he might be able to use the holstered weaponry he sported. A bead of sweat traced down from Skinner's hatband. He felt it run over his dust-caked features to his jaw.

'You figuring on killing me right here?'

Adams narrowed his eyes. 'I'm gonna give you a chance even though you don't merit it, sonny. I'm heading back out into the street to wait for you. If you don't come out after I count to fifty, I'll come back in with my guns blazing.'

'You can't do that,' Skinner protested fearfully.

'I can and I will!' The rancher took a backward step and leaned over to the man with the star pinned to his chest. He whispered a few words. 'Listen up. Go to the door and stand there, Don.'

'Just stand there?' Harper whispered back.

'Yep! Never take your eyes off him! Don't do nothing except watch him. Savvy?' Adams insisted.

Obeying the rancher's instructions, Harper turned and walked to the door of the large room.

When he reached it he turned and stared straight at Skinner.

Skinner looked totally confused. 'I don't want no truck with you.'

Adams winked. 'You either kill me or I kill you! There ain't no third way, sonny!'

Gene Adams inhaled deeply, then turned his back on the gunman. He began walking to where the marshal stood. He had only taken three steps when he saw the pained expression carved on Harper's face.

Even though he had his back to him, Adams knew that Skinner had risen with his gun in his hand.

As fast as a man half his age, Adams swung on his heels, drew both his guns, cocked their hammers and fired them at Skinner. A burst of fiery lead rocketed from the barrels of his .45s.

The brutal killer hit the wall hard. His gun fell from his hand. This time it was Skinner's turn to have bullet holes in his chest. Lifelessly he slid to the floor, leaving a red stain on the wall.

Gene Adams stood behind the gunsmoke as Harper ran to the body and quickly checked it. He looked up at the rancher who was sliding his Colts back into their holsters.

'Why'd you want me standing like a fool by the door, Gene?' he asked as he got back to his feet and returned to the ranches side. 'And how did you know he had gotten to his feet?'

'You told me, old friend. I knew your eyes would warn me when he was going for his gun, Don.' Adams sighed and began to turn. 'Never seen your eyes that big before!'

'That was a mighty big chance to take, Gene!' Harper gasped, rubbing his face. 'What if I'd blinked and not seen him rise with that hogleg in his hand?'

Gene Adams shrugged. 'Hell! I never thought of that!'

Harper sat down and picked up an abandoned glass of whiskey from a table. He downed it and shook his head. The lawman then watched as Adams walked silently towards the door. 'Where you going?'

'I gotta get my boys bedded down for the night. We got to get up early and I need me some shuteye, Don. I have to ride out to the Circle D tomorrow.'

'What?' The marshal pushed his hat off his sweat-soaked forehead.

Adams paused and smiled at his friend. 'Don't you remember? I only came here to buy me some horse flesh!'